A BEAST WITHIN

Aidan Lucid

Published by Aidan Lucid 2023

Book design by Aidan Lucid

Front cover illustration by Get Covers

For more information about Aidan Lucid and his books, go to www.aidanlucidauthor.com

Acknowledgements

I would like to thank the following people for their contributions to the production of this book:

- Dale L. Roberts and his fantastic self-publishing YouTube videos. They are very informative and have helped me no end on my author journey. Through his wisdom and advice often given in his weekly videos, Dale gave me the courage to self-publish my books. So, thank you, Dale!

- Kevin Cook for his superb military advice in Malcolm's nightmare in the 'Present Day-Boyd Household' section. Without Kevin's input from his time as a US soldier, that sequence would lack authenticity.

- **Editors:** Lisa at Hidden Gems and Olivia Logan for their eagle eyes and attention to detail.

- **Beta Readers:** Manusri, Megan, and Simona for your extremely helpful input.

- Tania at Get Covers for the superb front and back covers.

- God for giving me the gift of writing.

- And finally, you the reader, for purchasing *A Beast Within*. Thanks sincerely for supporting me and my work.

Prologue

A Year Ago

The Boyds' 1990 cream Wagoneer snaked its way along the winding road, flanked by pine trees like soldiers standing to attention. Malcolm tapped the steering wheel in time to Nirvana on the radio. The breeze from the inch of open window ruffled his raven-black hair.

Helena sat beside him, engrossed in a romance novel she had bought a week ago. She pulled back a wisp of brunette hair from her brown eyes.

Man, she's still beautiful. Malcolm thought remembering the day they met in high school, sixteen years ago. He was a little older than her, but when their eyes first locked, there had been an instant spark.

Guess she's got good genes, and I'm the lucky guy who married her.

Malcolm adjusted the rear-view mirror and glanced at their ten-year-old son, David, whose pale cheeks were a testament to a severe dose of anemia. His blond hair flopped forward as he stared, fixated, at his handheld console. Malcolm often watched Helena run her fingers through David's blond hair to help him drift off to sleep. He smiled at the mental image and turned off the radio, switching his attention to his son.

"Hey kiddo, all right back there?"

"Yeah, I'm good."

"Did you enjoy the last few days at Uncle Trevor's?"

Still entranced by his game, the boy didn't meet his father's gaze. "It was okay, I guess."

"Can't wait to get home, huh?" Malcolm continued.

"Mmm-hmm."

"You and me both, buddy," Malcolm mumbled. "How about we play a little game?"

"I'm already playing one."

"I was thinking more like 'I spy' or something."

David rolled his eyes. "That's for babies."

"And you're definitely not that anymore," Helena remarked, sneaking a quick grin at her husband.

Malcolm caught it, returning one of his own.

"Come on, we used to have so much fun. Exercise your brain rather than wasting it on that thing."

David didn't reply, instead returned to mashing the console's buttons, no doubt stringing together a killer knockout combo.

"Dr. Phil once said playing those games turns you into a zombie," Malcolm continued.

"You also said he's overpaid and full of crap," David returned.

Helena snickered, keeping her eyes on her book.

"A little help here," Malcolm whispered.

Putting the novel down, she turned around. "Don't use that language with your dad. It's rude."

"Sorry," David said in a half-hearted apology.

"Well, if you won't play, *I* will," Helena said. She faced forward, and looked for inspiration.

They turned a corner, and a long road stretched to the horizon. Parked on the shoulder was a brown Buick. Its driver, wearing a red flannel shirt, dirty black jeans, and a faded blue baseball cap was staring at the front left wheel.

"Okay, I spy with my little eye, something beginning with . . . C," Helena said.

David took a fleeting glance from his console before returning to beating up the bad guys. "Oh gee, I wonder what that could be," he said with a healthy dose of sarcasm.

As they approached the vehicle, Malcolm paid it more attention. "I think that guy might be in trouble. Maybe we should stop."

"Are you crazy? We don't know him. Just drive on."

"I can't just leave the guy there. He might need our help."

"We're out in the middle of nowhere. For all we know, he could be some psycho. Keep driving."

Malcolm looked in his rear-view mirror at the car and its driver growing smaller by the second. "I feel bad about leaving him there." He slowed to a stop, then shifted the stick into reverse.

"What are you doing? This is insane!" Helena protested as he reversed the Wagoneer.

"Yeah, but if anything happened to him, I'd never forgive myself. Besides, I can't just drive past him."

"Course you can. Just press the accelerator and go."

He brought the Wagoneer to a halt a few feet from the Buick and yanked up the handbrake. "I won't be long."

"Malcolm. *Malcolm*!" Helena hissed as he got out.

The stranger stood staring at the front left wheel, not acknowledging Malcolm's presence.

"Howdy, sir. Having car trouble?" he asked the chubby driver who appeared to be in his fifties.

"Got a flat. Can't change it with my back."

"I can do that if you like? Got a spare?"

"That's mighty kind of you, fella. Uh . . . yeah, in the trunk."

"Let me get my wrenching nut." Malcolm opened his own trunk and took out the tool. He kneeled down and began unscrewing the nuts. "You from around here?"

"The next town a few miles ahead. You?"

"We live about three hours away. Hartford Town. Ever heard of it?"

"Never, sir. Thanks for doing this. I'm starvin', I'm just waiting for my brother-in-law to come. Lazy bastard probably hasn't even left the house yet."

Malcolm chuckled. "Got one of those myself. Just don't tell her I said that."

"Yeah, God I'm hungry. Good thing you came along."

As Malcolm continued to unscrew the nuts on the flat tire, he noticed the driver walk a short distance away from him. Next, he heard the cracking of bones and popping sounds, as if joints were being dislocated. Low grunts soon transformed into growls.

Malcolm turned to look at the man but stood up, his jaw hung in terror.

"What…the…fu—" he uttered while retreating slowly to the

Wagoneer.

The stranger's shoulders grew wider as his shirt tore. Black fur replaced the man's chubby stomach.

"Holy crap!" Malcolm exclaimed.

The only reply he received was a quick snarl as the man turned around, no longer bearing a human face but a wolf's instead. Sharp, yellowed teeth dripped with saliva.

Helena's screams confirmed she saw it too.

"Hurry, Dad, get in," David cried, as tears streamed down his pale face.

Malcolm threw the wrenching nut, hitting the beast on the forehead. It staggered back, shaking its head, momentarily dazed.

Malcolm dashed into the driver's seat, his trembling hands fumbling for the keys. He jumped when the creature let loose a feral howl.

"Come on, start the damn car! David, honey, lock both doors and get down," Helena said.

The werewolf started walking towards the driver's door as the engine roared into life. As Malcolm pulled out onto the road, the beast ran after them, leaping into the air. A thud let them know he was on their roof.

"Oh, Christ. Lose him," Helena shouted.

Malcolm let loose a few expletives as an enormous paw smashed into his window. He swerved left and right to throw the monster off. Malcolm then slammed the brakes.

The beast rolled forward, digging his claws into the metal to keep himself on the car. Malcolm feared that they were so sharp, if the werewolf reached the windshield, it would slice or tear off the roof.

"Crap," cursed Malcolm as he drove again, unable to loosen the monster's grip and knock it off.

The tormentor crawled up towards the windshield. When it was on the hood, the creature went on all fours. He reached back his arm, ready to smash into the glass.

"Oh no you don't." Malcolm slammed on the brakes again, catapulting the beast off the Wagoneer. When it hit the ground, the werewolf tumbled and rolled around before coming to a stop, its left arm bent out of shape.

All the Boyds stared on in disbelief. Helena glanced down at her skirt; shame washed over her face as a circular patch of urine soaked her crotch.

Malcolm gave another quick glance in the mirror. David's face was whiter than normal, his eyes wide in horror. Malcolm grabbed his own right hand to stop it shaking.

They all jumped when the beast grunted again and raised its head, his bright green eyes locked menacingly on them.

Malcolm reversed the Wagoneer back a suitable distance away from their hellish tormentor.

"What are you doing?" Helena asked.

"Making sure he stays dead this time. David, cover your eyes." Malcolm floored the Wagoneer, speeding towards the werewolf.

Helena looked away.

Each of them hopped up and down as they rolled over it. Malcolm gave a cursory glance in the mirror while driving further from the beast while it stayed still.

Ferocious howling now swirled around the trees that lined both sides of the road.

"Is... Is there an- any more of them?" David stammered.

"Sure hope not," Malcolm replied, scanning everything they passed.

Without warning, another werewolf in a light red, ripped-up leather jacket jumped out in front of their car.

Malcolm swerved to avoid it while continuing on.

The monster ran at supernatural speed, jumping onto the Wagoneer's rear.

"David, get down!" Helena warned.

It bellowed a brief howl before driving its mammoth paw through the back window.

Glass rained on the boy as he covered his head. Helena screamed. Malcolm could see from the panic on her face that she wished she could shield their son.

Once again Malcolm swerved left and right, twisting the steering wheel hard in both directions to loosen the beast's grip. It continued to swipe at David, only catching thin air.

"Do something, Malcolm," Helena cried.

He stopped swerving, instead choosing to drive straight ahead. "Everybody, hang on!"

He slammed the brakes one last time while holding the steering wheel hard to the right. The Wagoneer spun around three times, like a cream metal whirlwind. On its third spin, the creature lost its grip, hitting the road with a loud thud.

As the Boyds came to a stop, Helena rolled her window down, emptying her stomach contents.

Malcolm cleared whatever shards of glass remained and stuck his head out. There, at a sickening 90-degree angle, was the werewolf's left leg sticking up. It howled in pain.

He ain't getting up in a hurry, Malcom thought. "You ready?" he asked Helena.

She nodded while wiping away any traces of vomit from her lips.

"You okay, buddy?" Malcolm said to David.

The boy nodded while still cowering with both hands covering his head.

"What about you, are you okay?" Helena asked her husband.

"Yeah, no scratches. I'll live."

"We gotta check David. I mean that was a friggin' werewolf."

"Not now. I ain't sticking around for another one of those things to attack." Malcolm pulled out onto the road and drove off. "Besides, I thought it was only if you're bitten that you'd…turn."

"But he could have scratches. We gotta pull over and check."

"We will. I just wanna get far from here first."

For several miles, Malcolm drove, his brown eyes darting left and right, surveying his surroundings for further dangers.

I think we're in the clear, he thought, finally satisfied that it was safe to pull over.

Both he and Helena undid their belts. They turned around, leaning in towards their son.

"Show me your hands," Helena said.

David sat up, turning them over and back. There were no scratches.

"Pull up your sleeves," Malcolm said.

David rolled them up but once more, there weren't any cuts or wounds.

"Oh, thank God," Helena said. "Okay, honey, we're done."

David rolled the sleeves of his white sweater down over both arms.

Malcolm's heavy breathing accompanied the sweat streaming down his forehead. The frightened man gave a rapid glance at his still-shaking hands. In his peripheral vision, he could see Helena's attractive face still sheet white, consternation fully setting in. She too grabbed her hands to stop them shaking.

"Did…that just really happen?" she asked, her gaze fixed straight ahead.

"Yeah…sure did. Werewolves, huh? They…exist."

"Guess so….and we just had to meet them."

"Never thought I'd see something like that in my life. Don't ever want to again." Helena put a hand up to her chest. "My damn heart's racing. Thank the Lord nobody got hurt."

"Amen to that. Let's just keep this between ourselves." At first, he directed this at Helena who nodded the affirmative before Malcolm added, "Do you hear me, buddy? This is our secret, okay?"

"Su— sure," David stammered. The boy's face was still ashen.

Malcolm wiped sweat lingering on his forehead. "Everybody belt up. The night ain't getting any younger."

When everyone had tied their safety belts, Malcolm continued as darkness quenched daylight. He hoped to leave this nightmare behind them, but this experience would not depart from their memory any time soon.

The Bank Job

Present Day

Jeremy Pegg turned the key in his apartment door and pushed it open. His heart sank when his amber eyes gazed inside it. He ran his hand through his acorn brown hair in semi-despair at the tiny living room. Beside it was an equally small en-suite kitchen.

I gotta go to Ikea when I get money, he thought staring at the sparse amount of furniture. Only a pea-green, food-stained sofa, a small coffee table, and one locker were all that was before him. The white wallpaper peeled in places.

Guess it beats being in prison the last four years, Jeremy thought. He picked up the suitcase of clothes Tamara, his mother, gave him when he got out. The last four years were hellish, being cooped in a cell, bunking with a dangerous gangbanger. This was something Jeremy wished he could erase like Thanos with a snap of his fingers. The shame it brought on his family, especially Tamara, always filled him with regret. He'd served four of a five-year sentence for armed robbery when he'd held up a grocery store. Every day he'd had to watch his back as certain inmates eyed him up and down.

When Tamara picked him up from prison, he had hoped it would be a journey home with her telling him how much she had missed him. Instead, he sighed with relief when the car ride ended, as Tamara berated him for his poor life choices.

"You gotta do something meaningful, Jeremy. You're not getting any younger," was one of her cutting remarks. Still, he was glad she got the apartment for him from an old friend who owed her a favor.

Jeremy fell onto the dusty, food-stained sofa. This time he was going to make the most of it. The disappointment in Tamara's eyes when she saw him was like someone plunging a knife through his heart.

"I'm sick of letting you down, Mom, I will do better. I promise," he muttered.

On his way to the apartment, Jeremy saw a father walking, holding his son's hand as they came out of the playground. Instantly, a part of him was envious. Damian, Jeremy's dad had passed away fifteen years ago - killed in a car accident. The absence of a father during his childhood had created a void in his heart that could never be filled.

Jeremy's phone rang, disturbing the silence. He slid it out of his pocket. Tamara's name was on the screen.

"Hey, Mom."

"So, what do you think of it?"

"Uh...nice," Jeremy lied.

"I know it's small but hey, it's a roof over your head, right?"

"Guess so. Thanks for setting this up."

"Glad I can help," Tamara said. "But I'm serious, Jeremy, time to get straight and make something of yourself."

He moved the phone away from his ears for a few seconds while rolling his eyes heavenwards. When Tamara was finished, Jeremy spoke again. "Yes, Mom, I know. And I will. I'm gonna really try."

"You better because if you go back in, we're done. I can't go through that again."

"Don't worry. I've no intention of going back."

"Better not. I left a surprise in a cupboard in the kitchen," Tamara said.

"You're the best. What would I do without you?"

"Not a whole lot. I gotta go. Cynthia's coming over later to play bridge. Ring you tomorrow. Don't forget you have that meeting in the morning with your PO. Don't be late. Need a drive?"

"Nah, it's only about a ten-minute walk from here so I'm good."

"All right. Catch ya later." Tamara hung up.

Meeting the Parole Officer, Ted Rollins, was not something Jeremy looked forward to. He heard from some inmates that Ted was not the most understanding of guys.

"Can't wait for it to be over," Jeremy muttered. He went into the kitchen to see what "surprise" his mother had left. Opening the cupboard revealed it was almost bare, save for three mugs she had loaned him and some dishes. A white envelope rested against one mug. Picking it up, it felt weighty.

Jeremy opened the envelope. Inside was $300 along with a note that said, "Buy yourself some clothes and stuff. Mom xx."

A lump formed in his throat. *Definitely gonna try to not let you down.*

***

Jeremy knocked on Ted's door twice. There was a curt, "Come in". He took a deep breath, bracing himself before entering.

The office was small and crowded with filing cabinets on both sides. The man's desk had bulky manila folders that contained case files for newly released ex-cons stacked high on it. A small, round silver ashtray with a smoldering cigarette was beside them. A window the width of Ted's broad frame was behind him.

"Take a seat," Ted said without looking up from Jeremy's folder. His sandy, side-swept hair was turning gray. He took out a pair of reading glasses from his faded yellow shirt pocket.

Jeremy sat on the chair.

"So, you were just released yesterday, that right?"

Jeremy nodded. "That's correct."

"I see and you've got somewhere to stay?"

"Yes, over by Arvington Place. A small one-bedroomed apartment."

"Get it by yourself?"

"Uh, no, sir. My mother knew a guy who was leasing it so..."

"Oh, still using mommy to help you. Nice."

Asshole, Jeremy thought trying with all his might to not say it.

Ted closed the folder. "Guess you know the drill by now. Find a job and work your way into being a responsible citizen in society again. Got any lined up?"

Jeremy shook his head. "No. I am looking, though."

"Find one. Fast. You're to check in with me at the start and end of every week. No alcohol or drugs. If you miss one appointment or don't return a call, I'm turning you in. No mixing with ex-cons and stay out of trouble. As for work," Ted opened a drawer and pulled out a newspaper. He had it opened on the classifieds page. One ad was circled in red. "I noticed this today."

Jeremy read over the advertisement. It was a janitor's position at a local high school. He surmised the pay was probably lower than the minimum wage and dealing with snot-nosed kids wasn't ideal. But if it meant repaying his debt to society, and his mother, putting up with ignorant teenagers was a small price to pay.

"Can I take this with me?" Jeremy asked, holding the paper.

Ted took it off him. "Hey, this isn't a charity. Get your own. I'm just throwing you a bone here."

Yup, definitely an a-hole. Again, he wrung his hands to prevent himself from saying something he'd regret.

"I showed this to two other guys today so don't hang around. Throw your name in for it." He opened a large black diary. Pushing down the button on his ball-point pen, Ted hovered it over the page as he asked, "Today is the tenth? So, meet me again in three days' time. Say 10am?"

"Yeah, sure."

"Good." Ted wrote the appointment date. "Hopefully you'll be working by then. And remember, if you're a no-show, I'm reporting you. Got that?"

"Yes sir. Loud and clear."

"Super." Ted closed the diary before putting down the pen. "Off you go."

Jeremy stood up, pushing in his chair. "Bye, Mr. Rollins."

"Sir."

Jeremy paused as he approached the door. "Huh?"

"It's goodbye, Mr. Rollins, *sir*," Ted corrected him.

Once more, he paused and took a deep breath, alleviating any anger that threatened to sneak to the surface. "Goodbye, Mr. Rollins, *sir*." He repeated, feigning a friendly smile. Once he was outside and the door was closed, Jeremy muttered a curse under his breath.

***

Later that evening, Jeremy phoned the school. A semi-cheerful re-
ceptionist helped set up an appointment with Principal Turner for
an interview the next day.

Tossing aside a book he was reading, Jeremy stared up at the
dirty white ceiling. Even though he relished being out of jail, this
was a prison of its own. Boredom was always quick to settle in.

Three knocks rapped on his door.

I wonder who that is? Jeremy approached it, slowly sliding
back the bolt lock, and opening the door a fraction of the way.

There standing with a six-pack of beer under his left muscular
arm was Stephen Andrews, a tall man in his thirties with a tight
crew cut. An attractive woman with spiky purple hair, in a black
leather jacket and torn denim jeans stood beside him.

"Stevie, how you doing?"

"Hey bud!" Stephen said, hugging him.

"How did you find me?"

"A friend of mine saw you living here and texted me. How
come you didn't reach out?"

"Once I got arrested, they confiscated my phone. I was gonna
email you just didn't get a chance."

"Sure, I understand. This is my girlfriend, Natalie."

Jeremy extended his hand. "Oh, hi, I'm Jeremy. Stephen talked
a lot about you when he visited me in prison."

She shook it. "Steve's been talking about you too, non-stop.
Like he never shuts up." Natalie had a cute Irish accent.

He forgot himself for a moment and stood back. "Sorry guys.
Come on in."

They entered; Stephen looked around.

"Welcome to my humble abode."

"Wow, talk about the bare necessities," Stephen remarked. "We
need to get you a new TV."

"I will once I start working. Can I get you guys a coffee, tea, or

15

even a glass for the beer?"

"No, we're good. Got a bottle opener?" Stephen asked.

"Yeah, sure." Jeremy took one from a drawer in the kitchen as his two guests sat down.

"So, when did you get out?" Natalie said.

"Oh, just yesterday. My..." He paused, not wanting to say that his mother arranged for him to get this apartment, "A friend knew a guy who was leasing this place and it's cheap, so I thought I'd bite."

"Cool." Stephen removed the cap off the bottle with the opener. Natalie did the same once he finished using it.

They talked for a while, sharing memories about their past. Jeremy eyed the last two bottles and resisted the urge to have another.

Stephen finished telling a story about a time they were almost caught stealing candy from a store. "And I'm standing there with like a pocket full of chocolate bars and another few stuffed inside my jacket when the owner sees me and is like, 'Hey, what you doin'? You gonna pay for those?' So, I'm there thinking I'm about to be busted when," Stephen pointed his bottle towards Jeremy, "Wise guy here comes around and says, 'There you are, Stevie. I've been looking all over for you! Sorry, sir, my brother's a little retarded.'"

They all laughed at that. Jeremy concluded the story, "I had to come along then and help him put all the stuff back. The owner was like, 'What the fuck?' We just ran like hell."

Again, Natalie and Stephen erupted in laughter, his right arm around her. Jeremy smiled, remembering them running for their lives before the cops were called.

"Yeah, good times. He saved my ass more than I can count," Stephen added.

"Seems like you boys were pretty close," Natalie commented.

"Yeah, like brothers," Jeremy said.

Both he and Stephen clinked bottles to that.

"This dude kept me sane when I was inside, visiting a couple o' times a month."

Jeremy remembered the first time he met Stephen. The boy

wore hand-me-down clothes that were bigger than he was. No other kid would play with him, so Jeremy felt sorry for Stephen. He introduced himself, both hitting it off straight away.

"So got any work lined up?" Stephen asked.

"I've got an interview tomorrow. A school janitor."

His friend frowned. "Oh, wow, that sucks. Don't get me wrong, hope it goes well for you but yeah, hate dealing with kids."

"I'm not exactly thrilled about it either but hey, money's money, right?"

They nodded in agreement.

"Seriously though, it's good to see you outside of a cell, man. Missed you," Stephen said.

"Yeah, missed you too." They clinked bottles again. The men talked for the next few hours about old times and scrapes they barely got out of.

***

Jeremy opened the double doors to Baxterton High School and looked around for a teacher to ask where the principal's office was. He found one coming out of a classroom, a tall blonde who resembled his French teacher back in the day. She was locking a door.

"Uh hi. Can you tell me where I can find Principal Turner's office?"

"Yeah, sure. It's down the hall, take a right and it's the last door on the left."

"Great, thanks." Jeremy followed her directions.

Standing here brought back memories of his school days. Of the many times he and Stephen made trips to the then principal's office. This time it was different.

Jeremy was about to knock when Principal Turner opened the door. "Oh, yes?" he said matter-of-factly, snobbery in his tone.

"My name's Jeremy Pegg. We have an interview today."

"That's right. I forgot. Since you're here, come in." Turner, an impish man with black hair in a side part style and a stubble goatee, moved back, opening the door further.

Jeremy took a seat.

"You have a resumé on you?" Turner asked while shutting the door.

"Yes, sir. Here." Jeremy placed the sheet of A4 paper on the desk.

"Let's have a look," Turner replied while sitting down and picking it up. His eyes moved left to right, scanning each line until he stopped midway. "I see there's a four-year gap. Why's that?"

Jeremy felt his mouth go dry. This was the part he dreaded the most. "Well, sir, I was..." He cleared his throat, quickly trying to find the words to answer it that would make him look less like a criminal.

"Come on, man, it's not a hard question to answer. Out with it."

"Truth is...I was incarcerated for that time."

Turner sat back in the chair, regarding him with a suspicious gaze. "What were you arrested for?" His tone, although never welcoming since they met, now became harsher.

"For robbing a grocery store with a firearm. I got an early release for good behavior."

"Hmm...I see." Turner held him in a long intense stare.

Great. I blew it, Jeremy thought, expecting the interview to end.

The principal sat forward, reading over the rest of Jeremy's resumé, shoving the page away from him when he was finished.

"You're punctual so that's one thing going for you. But the problem we have here, Mr. Pegg—"

"I'm not getting—"

"Don't interrupt me."

Jeremy felt like he was fifteen years old again, about to receive a scolding for truancy. He balled both fists under the desk, fighting the urge to remind Turner that he wasn't a student.

"As I was saying, we don't usually hire ex-cons here. Thing is, we have a janitor, but he can only work until three. There needs to be after-school work done like cleaning toilets and some classrooms. You're the only person who applied." Again he sat back, twiddling his thumbs while pondering. "My dad used to be a screw in San Quentin before we moved here. He had a saying that even the lowest of the low deserves a second shot in life."

Gee thanks for your high opinion of me, Jeremy thought.

"So, I'm going to do just that with you, Mr. Pegg."

Jeremy's heart almost leapt with joy.

"Can you start this evening? As in, right now?"

Jeremy was stunned into silence, unable to utter a reply for a few seconds until he quickly gathered his thoughts. "Um...yes, sure!"

He was about to put out his hand to shake Turner's in gratitude when the principal said, "You're an ex-con so I suppose you got nothing better to do anyway."

Jeremy kept it by his side, forcing a smile, and stayed calm. "Thanks so much for this. I won't let you down."

"See that you don't. I'll be keeping a close eye on you, though."

"That's okay, sir. I'll just do my job," Jeremy replied.

"Drop in your bank details tomorrow and I'll have payroll set you up."

"Thanks. I will."

For the next hour, Jeremy received a tour of the school and was shown the janitor's room. He changed into the janitor uniform and went from classroom to classroom to check if they needed to be cleaned. There were some photocopied handouts left on the ground and a few spillages in two chemistry labs but nothing too arduous.

That was before he came to the toilets.

At the entrance, the pungent smell of urine and excrement greeted him hard. Graffiti was scrawled on some cubicles, a pool of fresh urine was beneath one toilet, and a moist turd was stuck on the side of another.

Yup, you just gotta love kids. He sighed and began cleaning the mess.

***

The piping hot pepperoni and cheese pizza not only smelled but looked delicious. It was a welcome distraction from the disgusting job of cleaning toilets earlier. The stomach-churning stench of piss and shit still lingered up his nose. He knew it would take a few hours for it to disappear.

Lifting a slice, some of the cheese slid off it, falling back into the box. Jeremy took one bite; the pizza tasted like heaven in his mouth. The cheese melted on his tongue while each slice of pepperoni had a spicy zing to it.

Jeremy's dinner was disturbed by his cell ringing. Stephen's name was on the screen. He had given Jeremy his number before leaving the apartment yesterday.

"Hey Stevie. What's up?"

"Not much. Listen, can we meet? Me and Nat have something we wanna talk to you about."

"No offence but I can't meet with other ex-cons in public. My PO will bust my ass if I do."

"Shoot, I forgot. Okay, what if we met in private?"

"Like where?"

Stephen paused for a moment. Then he conferred with Natalie in the background before switching back to Jeremy. "How about the alleyway at the back of your building?"

"I don't know...if anybody sees us—"

"Who's gonna see us and rat you out?" Stephen butted in.

Jeremy thought about it for a moment and replied, "All right. It'll be a quick meeting, okay? What do you wanna talk about anyway?"

"We'll tell you when we meet up. Say around eight in the evening? We'll be parked there."

"Fine but it'll have to be quick. I'm not taking any chances."

"Got it. See you then and don't worry, everything's gonna be fine."

Hope so, Jeremy thought while hanging up.

At eight o'clock the following evening, Jeremy made his way to meet Stephen, taking the back door route, ensuring nobody would see him. He stood in the middle of the alleyway, glancing around for the car. One flashed its headlights twice. Jeremy knew that this was Stephen's signal.

He hurried to the spot where his friend had parked. As Jeremy got closer, he could see that Natalie was also there, sitting in the front.

Jeremy sat in the back of the 1999 Chevy Camaro, silently admiring its cream-colored leather seats at first. "Nice car. Where did you steal it from?"

"Steal it? Jeremy, I'm shocked," he said, feigning offence. "No, I actually bought it off a guy a year ago."

"It's a beaut'. Real nice." Jeremy felt the seat, smooth to the touch. He wondered if Stephen and Natalie had broken it in yet. "So, what do you wanna talk about?"

Natalie and Stephen exchanged a nervous glance before he spoke up. "Me and Nat are about to do a job and we want you in on it."

"Are you serious?"

"Like a heart attack," Stephen replied. "We've been planning this for months. We could use a tech guy to do some hacking. I don't know anyone better than you."

"Where are you gonna hit?"

Natalie answered this time, "Can't exactly say right now, Jers, until we know you're in."

"So, you think I'm gonna rat you out? Thanks for that. Good talk." He opened the door and was about to leave when Stephen caught his arm.

"No, that's not what she means. We don't want to tell you because we don't want you getting arrested if you're not gonna be involved. Plausible deniability and all that."

Jeremy stared at him for a long moment and closed the door. "Guess that makes sense. I only just got out, though. I wanna go straight this time. No more screw-ups or goofing around. Plus, I promised my mother I wouldn't go back to the old life."

"Bit of a momma's boy, are ya?" Natalie joked.

Jeremy frowned. Stephen glared at her, giving his girlfriend a look that said she wasn't helping matters.

"Sorry," Natalie apologized half-heartedly.

Stephen jumped in. "Look, we respect that, we do. But cleaning high schools and other crappy jobs, that's beneath you, Jeremy. You're so much better than this!"

"Yeah, maybe, but I'm still going straight. No more crime for me."

Stephen sighed in defeat. "Okay, guess it's your choice. We'll give you three days to decide."

"Appreciate that but won't be changing my mind anytime soon."

Natalie turned around to face him again. "Well, Jers, you have our number if you do."

"Thanks." Jeremy glanced around, trying to see if anyone was about. Looking in both directions, he bolted to the building's rear door.

Stephen's offer was tempting but Jeremy didn't want to be a criminal anymore. From now on, he wanted to do things the honest way, even if it meant earning wages that were less than he hoped for.

***

The bus pulled up at Jeremy's stop, opening its doors to let him in. He loved to walk but the relentless rain impeded on his daily exercise regime. Jeremy took a seat at the back. The last bus ride he was on was to prison. Feelings of shame, guilt, and remorse rose to the surface as he remembered staring out the barred windows, wishing to be anywhere but there.

I got a chance to make things right so I'm gonna take it, he thought.

Reaching into his pockets, he took out a pair of earphones and slipped them into his ears. Plugging the jack mic into its slot on his cell, Jeremy tapped an app that brought up his favorite radio station. Music filled his ears and he bopped his head to its beat.

The bus came to another stop. This time an old, haggard vagrant with tattered jeans and a faded lime-colored shirt, stepped on.

He slipped the driver a few coins. His beard was long, dirty with some hairs being knotted. Soot was also spread on his face. He coughed while taking his seat.

Jeremy's stop was next, so he took out the earphones and stuffed them back into his jacket pocket. The vagrant coughed heavily again, leaning forward he placed a hand to his chest. The other gripped the seat in front of him.

"Are you okay, sir?" Jeremy asked.

The man nodded, giving a thumbs-up while still coughing. He then stopped to wipe the drool from his mouth.

Jeremy slid the cell into his pocket and was about to stand up when the old man resumed coughing, this time keeling over.

Crap, Jeremy thought, rushing to the hobo's side. "Sir, are you okay?" There was no response; his eyes were closed. "Sir, can you hear me?" he shook him this time, noticing that others looked on too. Putting a finger to the hobo's neck, Jeremy felt for a pulse; there was none. "Somebody call an ambulance. This man's stopped breathing," he shouted.

The bus driver quickly pulled over, phoning for emergency medical help. Jeremy opened the man's shirt. He stood back as a revolting stench assaulted his nose. Jeremy gave chest compressions four times and breathed into the man's mouth.

On the fifth time, the hobo responded by spluttering twice and inhaling a deep breath.

Oh thank God, Jeremy thought. The wailing of ambulance sirens as it arrived was another welcomed sound. Two EMTs jumped out and ran onto the bus. He stepped back as they took over. One asked Jeremy what happened, and he explained.

"He's a hero," Jeremy heard a woman whisper to her friend.

"He saved that man's life," another murmured to a passenger in front of him.

Soon they carried the old vagrant off on a gurney to their ambulance.

As Jeremy got off, he had to swallow a spit of emotion when all the passengers applauded his efforts earlier. A feeling of pride swelled inside of him as he waved goodbye to everyone when he left.

As Jeremy walked into the high school, the good feeling didn't last long.

There, standing with folded arms and pointing to his watch was Principal Turner. "You're ten minutes late. Why?" he snapped.

"Sorry, Mr. Turner, but an old guy collapsed on the bus on my way over here. I had to do CPR on him."

"Well, aren't you quite the caped crusader?" the principal said sarcastically. "I don't care if your own mother drops dead or the sky falls down around us. At quarter past four I expect your ass to be here doing your job, not out saving the world! Understood?"

"But, sir, I had to. The man would've—"

"I don't care, Pegg! You're to be here on time because if you're late again, get a job somewhere else. Now get to it." Principal Turner stormed off to his office, leaving Jeremy to stand in amazement, shaking his head in disbelief.

"Un-friggin'-believable," he muttered while walking to the janitor's room.

***

The next evening, Jeremy arrived ten minutes early. Turner waited for him by the janitor's room. When Jeremy approached it, the principal offered him a thin smile and walked away.

What, no lectures today? Lucky me, he thought while taking out a sweeping brush.

He started on the halls, working his way to the toilets. On the football field, he could hear the coach blowing his whistle, shouting orders and advice, and telling players to tighten their defenses. It brought him back to his school days when he used to play basketball. His coach singled Jeremy out every time he made a mistake, always taking Jeremy aside and berating him for his poor dribbling and passing skills.

An hour later while on a five-minute break, Jeremy ate a chocolate bar and drank it down with a can of soda. Three tall jocks each carrying gym bags, walked past him. One threw up an empty soda bottle and caught it. When he was passing a trash can, he 'accidentally' missed when trying to throw the bottle in. It bounced on the floor twice and remained there.

"Oops, sorry. My bad," mocked the teen. His friends laughed with him as they walked on.

"What a loser," another one remarked as they left school.

Nothing ever changes. Jocks are still dicks. Jeremy threw his own bottle and the kid's into the can while casting hateful eyes on the arrogant teens.

That night, while at home, he thought about Turner's treatment of him and how little he was appreciated in his new job. A part of Jeremy was tempted to take Stephen up on his offer.

He took out the phone, scrolling through the contact list comprising of only three names. A finger hovered over Stephen's.

Any other life would be better than this.

Then Tamara's words replayed in his mind, "If you go back in, we're done. I can't go through that again." The mental images of his mother crying and walking away in disgust were enough to make Jeremy put away his phone.

***

Jeremy sat in the café waiting for his order. It was dusty with some tables not being cleaned off properly. Coffee circle stains and crumbs from food were on them.

Should I even eat here? A shiver of abhorrence went through his body as he imagined cockroaches running wild in the kitchen and rats having a buffet late at night. The only thing that enticed him to stay was the price of food and drinks. They were the lowest in town.

The waitress smiled as she served Jeremy his coffee and Danish pastry. It was a long time since he'd had one of these.

"Thank you, ma'am," he said, eyeing the pastry with delight. Jeremy used some of Tamara's money and knew a luxury like this would only be a once-off until he got another job.

"Would you like today's paper to read while you're having that,

25

sir?" she asked.

"Uh, yeah, sure."

She took one from an empty table. "There you go. Enjoy."

"Thanks." Jeremy sipped his coffee while flicking through the pages. He stopped at a headline that read, "Hero Saves Man's Life on Bus". There were a few paragraphs detailing what happened. A black-and-white picture of the hobo was beside the story. They hailed a male who matched Jeremy's description as a 'hero'. He read the entire article twice, a proud smile finding its way onto his face on a second read-through.

"I owe that man big time. Thank you, whoever you are", was the part Jeremy loved reading the most.

Just glad I could do something good for a change. With a flick of his wrist, Jeremy checked his watch. There were another twenty minutes left before his second meeting with Ted.

Maybe he might give me some credit for saving that hobo's life. Then he rolled his eyes.

Who am I kidding? he scoffed.

***

Smoke from Ted's cigarette slowly drifted into the air, giving an unpleasant odor. Jeremy had to spray a lot of antiperspirants on his clothes after his last visit, unable to afford to take them to a launderette.

Ted glanced over Jeremy's file.

Just hope he hurries up this time, he thought, waving the smoke away.

"So, you got that janitor job?" Ted asked.

"Yes, sir, I did."

"Good. It's refreshing to see an ex-con be productive so quickly."

Jeremy didn't know if this was a compliment or an insult. "Um...thanks." *I think.*

"You looking for other work? I mean, those hours ain't gonna be enough to support you."

"Yes."

"Well try harder." Ted opened a drawer, pulling out a Breathalyzer. "You know what this is?"

"I do."

"Last month we've been authorized to use these for alcohol testing. So, blow into it."

Jeremy leaned forward, blowing into the device. The parole officer took it back, waiting for a beep. "You're good." He ticked a box on the page. "Gold star for you," he added dryly.

Jeremy gave an uneasy chuckle.

"I read about someone saving an old guy on a bus yesterday. The man sounded a lot like you. Was it?"

"Uh, yes, Mr. Rollins. I learned First Aid a few years ago."

"Guess it was a case of the right guy at the right place at the right time, huh?"

Is he actually giving me praise?

"Next thing you'll be wearing a cape and climbing trees to save cats," Ted joked with a sarcastic sneer.

Again, Jeremy wrung his hands to stop himself from saying something he would regret. *I really hate this dude.*

***

As Jeremy mopped the high school's floors, what Ted said earlier played on his mind.

Will the guy ever give me a break? I'm really trying here!

A person talking on their phone as they neared him, caught his attention. A tall, stout man in his late forties, walked into Jeremy's view. He was on his cell phone and held an empty bottle of water in his right hand.

"Yeah, the kids are getting stronger every week. I feel we've got a great chance of winning the Championship this year. That McCullough boy can run. Scored three touchdowns in the last game." He glanced at the clock on the wall. "Speaking of running, I gotta go. Talk to you tomorrow."

That must be the coach, Jeremy surmised before returning to mop the floors.

Coach whistled a tune while walking past him. Jeremy looked up. There, standing on a table was the man's empty bottle, a few feet away was the trash can.

"Uh, excuse me, sir," Jeremy called out.

The coach turned around. "Yeah?"

"Can you please put your bottle into the trash can?"

"Isn't that your job?"

"But it's right there." Jeremy pointed to it.

"Then you do it. Isn't that what you're paid to do around here?"

Jeremy stared on speechless while the coach left, astounded by the man's arrogance.

What a d-bag! He dumped the bottle a little too forcefully in anger, making a loud clatter as he threw it in.

An hour later while Jeremy put the mop bucket into the janitor's room, he overheard two teachers talking in a nearby classroom. Its door was slightly ajar. He recognized the voice of Principal Turner.

"So, who's the new guy?" a female teacher asked.

"The janitor?" Principal Turner replied.

"Yeah, him."

"His name's Jeremy Pegg. Life's been kind of hard, so I threw him a bone."

Wow, maybe he's nicer than I thought.

"Looks kinda shifty if you ask me," the other teacher said.

"Between us," As the principal continued, he lowered his voice but it was still audible enough for Jeremy to hear. "And this stays between us."

"Uh-huh," the female teacher said.

"He's an ex-con. Looking to turn his life around. My dad used to be a guard and told me stories about prisoners trying to go straight. So, I felt I had to give him some crumbs, you know, something to cling to."

"Very noble of you," the woman replied in a voice of approval. "Like my mom used to say, 'Even the dumbest dogs deserve some love'."

Turner laughed before agreeing. "Yes, well said."

Jeremy leaned up against the wall. To him, it was as if he got sucker punched. *Is that what they think of me, some lost little puppy? Throwing me 'a bone'?*

With his head lowered and shoulders slouched in utter dejection, he left the high school.

That night he tried to watch YouTube videos on his phone and read a book to take his mind off the conversation earlier, but nothing worked. That woman's harsh words still rang in his ears.

No matter what I do, I'll always be crapped down on by assholes like him.

He picked up a picture of Tamara and held it. Jeremy's eyes welled up as he stared at her.

"Sorry, Mom. I really tried but they're never gonna accept me. I'll always be some charity case or joke to them."

Jeremy picked up his cell. There was only one call left to make. He hit Stephen's name. After two rings, his friend picked up.

"Yo, Stevie, is that job offer still open?"

"Sure is."

"Can you get me a high-spec laptop and a monitor?"

"Uh-huh, if that's what you need."

"Then I'm in."

***

Jeremy sat in the back seat with the laptop on his lap. Stephen sat in the front. He could sense his friend's nervousness with the constant drumming of fingers on the steering wheel. Jeremy's heart thumped faster than usual but he kept a calm face.

With a few keystrokes, the screen was divided into four parts. He was inside the bank's CCTV mainframe, having a clear view of each camera's feed.

"All right, I'm inside. When do you want them to stop?"

Stephen checked his watch and said, "Twelve fifty-nine pm. Five minutes."

"Okay, got it. Are you sure your guy can come through?"

29

"Yup, I trust him. He said he took care of the guard watching the cameras."

With his curiosity piqued, Jeremy asked, "Why, what did he do?"

"He slipped something in the dude's coffee. He should be taking a long nap by now."

"Let's hope so," Jeremy replied.

"One more thing, we're gonna use codenames while inside. You're 'Fred' and Natalie's 'Flamingo'."

"Oh, I bet she loved that name," Jeremy joked.

"Yeah, like a poker up the ass," Stephen quipped with a half-smile.

Jeremy watched each minute pass until it was 12:59pm. "Here goes nothin'," Jeremy said. After hitting two keys, the camera feeds went dead. "They're down."

For three days, he worked on creating a RAT (Remote Access Trojan) to stop the CCTV cameras for twenty minutes. Their inside man planted the virus into the system through a USB flash drive, which allowed Jeremy to switch them off.

"Good, now go. Nat's already inside. Just like we discussed," Stephen said.

"In, get the money and out. No screwing around," Jeremy interrupted. "Yeah, I know."

"Then go, go, go."

Jeremy ran to the front door, stopping to shove his gun deeper into his jacket pocket.

He opened the door. Two security guards in black clothing were at the bank's entrance. Glock 19s were holstered to their hips. They nodded in greeting. He nodded back. There were three lines of people waiting to see tellers. He joined the first.

The bank had gleaming marble floors. There were four CCTV cameras, one at each corner. Their red light which normally would be blinking, was dead. Line dividers consisting of a red rope hanging between gold posts separated three lines of customers. The window frame for each teller was made of thick oak surrounding a sheet of Plexiglas.

Natalie was in the line beside him. A mini Irish flag was on the lapel of her leather jacket. She winked at Jeremy.

"Yo, Joe, I'm taking an early lunch break. See you in an hour," one security guard said to the other.

"Got it. Have a good one."

Jeremy watched as the man unlocked a door to the far left marked, "Staff only" and went inside. After a few minutes, he emerged in a navy windbreaker. The Glock was no longer holstered to his hip. Joe locked the bank doors as his colleague left.

Natalie's cold dark eyes locked with Jeremy's. An unnerving smile on her face let him know it was time. They both put on what first appeared like fisherman caps.

Jeremy was next in line. When he and Natalie glanced to see if the coast was clear, they revealed that the caps were actually ski-masks now pulled down over their faces. Then they each pulled out a handgun.

"Get on the ground. Nobody tries anything stupid," Natalie said in her thick Dublin brogue while waving her weapon.

All the customers and tellers screamed, laying face down, covering their heads with both hands.

Joe ran up to Natalie, his Glock drawn.

"Head to the vault," she commanded.

"On it, but let me get the bags first." He ran to the locker area the other guard went into earlier. He came out with three duffel bags, handing one of them to Jeremy. Then Joe rushed to a door leading to where the weeping and whimpering tellers stood. He took out a key and opened it. A few seconds later Joe unlocked another door that was behind the tellers.

Natalie stepped forward. "Joe, get the manager."

He ran out and pulled a balding man in his early fifties up from the floor. "Get up!" he barked.

"All right, all right," the bald man said. The manager shoved his spectacles up as they slid down his nose a little. "Thomas" was on the bronze name tag attached to a black suit jacket.

"Fred, go with Thomas here to the back. When the vault's

open, you and Joe pack as many bags as you can." She stepped forward, shoving the cold nozzle under Thomas's double chin. "And yous better cooperate or you're about to have a terrible day. Know what I mean?"

"Ye- yes, s- sure. Ju- just don't hurt me."

"Let's go. Move." Joe grabbed the back of Thomas's collar and shoved him towards the vault door.

Jeremy fell in behind them.

With a trembling hand, Thomas entered a code on the keypad. He punched in the correct number on the keypad and each key lit up in a milky white light.

"Thanks," Joe said before pistol-whipping him hard across the face.

Thomas crumpled to the ground.

"Was that really necessary?" Jeremy asked.

"Shut up and start packing," Joe ordered while pulling open the large vault door.

Natalie's eyes roved over every customer lying down, watching any suspicious movements of their hands.

"This will be all over in a minute. If nobody tries anything then we'll all go home happy."

In the corner of Natalie's eye, she saw a sandy-haired woman moving towards a red fire alarm. She swung the gun on her. "Hey, don't even think about it, love." Natalie walked briskly towards the side entrance door to where the tellers were.

"Screw this," the teller said, punching the glass.

The alarm blared. Intermittent screams erupted from some customers.

"You dozy cow!" Natalie yelled, kicking open the entrance door, and unloading two slugs into the teller.

More hysterical cries broke out.

"You two are next if you're daft enough to try anythin'. Right?"

Both women nodded their heads frantically.

Come on, lads. Hurry up, Natalie thought.

Jeremy almost leapt with fright as the alarm started ringing.

"Damn," he exclaimed.

"How much do you have?" Joe asked.

"About two hundred grand in each bag."

Joe stuffed another stack of cash into his. "It'll have to do. C'mon."

Jeremy grabbed the heavy bags.

Joe was the first to exit the vault area, meeting Natalie at the teller's entrance.

"That all you got?" she asked.

"Yup. We need to get outta here, as in right now," Joe advised.

"He's right. Cops will swarm the place any minute," Jeremy added.

"Guess you're right. Feck it. Come on," Natalie said.

Joe ran to an exit door several feet away from the staff locker room. After he shouldered it open, a dull unpainted side wall of a building and an overfilled dumpster were all that could be seen. Joe dashed to the right.

"Fred, you're next," Natalie shouted.

He bolted out, Stephen already had the engine running. Jeremy put his bags in the trunk before sitting in the back next to Joe. He sighed in relief, taking off the mask.

Moments later, Natalie got into the car, sitting in the front and removed hers too.

Just as Stephen was about to speed away, Natalie said, "Hold it." She pulled out her handgun again, aiming it at Joe. "You can get out here."

"Whoa...hold on a second, you wouldn't have been able to pull this off without me," he replied.

"Does this look like a democracy or somethin'? Get out." She removed the safety.

"What are you doing, Natalie?" Jeremy said, puzzled.

"Getting rid of dead weight," she snapped back as Joe exited the Camaro.

"Rot in hell, bitch," the security guard roared back.

"You first, dipshit." Natalie fired one shot, getting her former accomplice between the eyes. Blood sprayed as the bullet exited his skull. "Right, go, go, go!"

"You knew about this, Stevie?" cried Jeremy in exasperation.

"Hey, less chit-chat and more drivin'," Natalie ordered.

Stephen reversed and turned around. Just as he was driving into the flow of traffic, Jeremy paled when he made an unwelcome discovery.

"Guys, we're on CCTV."

"What?" Natalie said, turning around in shock.

Pointing over his shoulder, Jeremy said, "There was a CCTV camera at the side of a building opposite the bank. It was pointed at our car."

"Everybody just stay calm," Stephen advised. "We'll be out of town in five minutes."

Jeremy didn't share his optimism knowing it would be longer than that before they were far from here. They were now caught in a long line of tailbacks. For all three thieves, it felt like the lights stayed red for an eternity.

A police cruiser pulled up beside their car. Jeremy tried to look calm and not have a pensive or worrisome expression.

Stephen noticed it too when he said, "All right, guys, play it cool. They can't be onto us that quickly."

"I wish these bleedin' lights would change," Natalie moaned.

Jeremy stared straight ahead, trying to avoid the gaze of any police officer. Many times he felt his eyes being drawn to the cruiser and pulled them back, focusing on the rear of Natalie's head. But after several minutes of fighting it, Jeremy capitulated.

He focused on an officer who was driving the cruiser.

The officer didn't return his stare at first but then gave an unnerving sideways glance. He quickly studied Jeremy and then the car. His attention was drawn to the radio and he stopped inspecting. Picking up the speaker microphone, the cop looked ahead as he talked.

Suddenly the man stared at the car again, his face awash with alarm.

"Uh...guys, I think we've been made," Jeremy announced.

"What makes you think that?" Natalie asked.

"He's looking at us like he recognizes the car."

Traffic moved as the lights turned green.

"About time," Stephen said.

Now all three jumped when the cruiser's sirens were turned on.

"Shit. Drive Steve!" Natalie barked.

"Hold on." Stephen slammed on the accelerator, passing through all the cars, and weaving in between different lanes of traffic. Although Jeremy had his safety belt on, he felt like a pinball being tossed around in a machine with all the sharp turns Stephen made.

"Easy, Stevie, I'm gonna puke," Jeremy said.

"God's sake, man, I'm trying to lose the cops!"

From the driver glancing to the side mirror every ten to fifteen seconds, Jeremy noticed beads of sweat trickling down Stephen's forehead. Jeremy was perspiring too.

As the Camaro passed a junction and Stephen drove through a red light, two more cruisers joined in the chase.

"Oh great. That's all we need," Stephen grumbled.

"This just keeps gettin' better and better," Natalie added.

Jeremy had to fight the onset of motion sickness as his friend continued to overtake cars, cutting in front of others to try and evade the police. A cyclist came to a halt as Stephen swerved to avoid him while straightening up the car again.

Once the second lane was clear, one of the new cruisers pulled up beside their vehicle. The cop driving it motioned for them to pull over.

"Ain't gonna happen," Stephen said.

"Jers, you got your gun on you?" Natalie asked.

"Yeah, why?"

"Fire off a few shots. Get rid of these wankers."

"Are you kidding me?" Jeremy shouted back.

Natalie half turned around. "Does this face look like it's jokin'?"

"Jeremy's right. We can't risk shootin' up here," Stephen interjected.

Jeremy could see his friend's gaze suddenly switched to an eighteen-wheeler coming from a side lane up ahead.

"I got a better idea." Stephen increased his speed again, the cruiser still parallel with the car.

Just as they were passing another set of traffic lights, Stephen rammed the cruiser, sending it straight into the lorry. The sickening sound of glass breaking, and metal being crunched was heard as two vehicles collided. Stephen swerved left hoping to throw off the cruisers, but they continued on their tail.

"How far till the state line?" he asked, exiting the city and onto the long highway.

"I think about another ten minutes," Jeremy answered. "Do you think we can make it?"

Stephen constantly glanced into the rear-view mirror being lit up by flashing red and blue lights. "It's either that or prison."

"I don't fancy being anyone's bitch in there," Natalie said.

Jeremy gulped when the two remaining cruisers were no longer in single file but flanked both sides of the Camaro.

"These guys ain't playin' around. We need to do something fast. I can't ram them here," Stephen said.

Natalie patted her jacket where the gun was concealed. "I think it's time for Plan B."

"We can't shoot our way outta this, Nat. We're out-gunned," Jeremy pointed out.

"Right now, it's the only way out," she snapped back.

Everyone in the car jumped when a command came from one of the cruisers' speakers.

"Pull over! This is your only warning. Comply now or we'll be forced to shoot."

"Plan B it is," Natalie said, removing the gun, keeping it low, out of the cop's line of sight. She rolled down her window.

"What are you doing?" Stephen asked.

"Don't see another way out of it," she said.

Jeremy's heart pounded harder than ever before. In the next five minutes, he knew one of two things was going to happen. Either they were gonna shoot their way to freedom or die trying.

Natalie released the safety and eyed the vehicle on her left. She aimed the weapon, firing two shots.

Her first penetrated the windshield and the second made contact with the driver. The police car veered away from them onto the sandy, rocky terrain.

"Woohoo! Nice one, Nat," Stephen said.

Natalie stroked the gun. "One down, one to go."

The last police car now fell behind.

A shot shattered the rear window, cutting short Natalie and Stephen's celebrations.

Jeremy ducked for cover while Stephen roared.

Natalie stared at her boyfriend's wounded arm. "Oh shite. They got ya."

"No, I think it's just a flesh wound," he assured her.

"It's time to lose these bastards. Do you remember the move we did two years ago in Texas?" Natalie asked.

"The spin and shoot?" Stephen said, eyeing her curiously.

"That one. Yeah. Ready to do it again?"

"Why don't I like the sound of this?" Jeremy said, his voice a few octaves higher.

"Just keep down, Jers," Natalie advised. "Ready Steve?"

He nodded.

"Speed up. Get some distance," she said.

Stephen pressed the accelerator, putting a gap between both vehicles.

"Now!" she yelled.

Stephen performed a hard left handbrake turn. The Camaro skidded sideways as Natalie unloaded her clip, shells ejected from the chamber. Two bullets hit the cop in the front passenger's seat. Blood sprayed the windshield before the brakes screeched.

"We did it!" Natalie announced.

"Nice one," Stephen complimented her. "Now let's get the hell out of here."

Once more, he pressed the accelerator but this time, they all breathed a sigh of relief and knew they were safe as they crossed state lines.

At least for now.

The Boyd Household

Malcolm lay in bed, tossing and turning, his forehead drenched with sweat. Ever since that frightening encounter a year ago, he experienced the same dream a couple of times every week. In this nightmare, he was back to his old life as a soldier - Sergeant Boyd. It was 2012 and he was in Afghanistan, driving an M1151 High-Mobility Multipurpose Wheeled Vehicle, part of a convoy on patrol with his Humvee taking the lead. Balmy heat made the ride even more stifling with perspiration being collected under his helmet. There are two other soldiers with him, Corporal Rodriguez, a Latina in her early twenties in the other front seat, one of the best shooters in his platoon. Manning the turret gun is Private Damian Walsh, a rugged thirty-something of Irish descent.

"So, you think of your girl much?" Rodriguez asked, an M4 Carbine rifle was at her side.

"Now and again. What about you? Is Jake on your mind all the time?"

"Course. Miss him like hell. Bet you're hard up like he is?" she asked with an expanding grin.

Malcolm didn't answer at first, shamefaced.

"Aw, look at you, sir, all embarrassed," Rodriguez teased, playfully hitting his arm.

"What makes you think he's not getting it somewhere else?" Malcolm quipped.

"Hey, he'd never do that."

"Why, was he an altar boy or something growing up?"

The woman's tone changed from teasing to being stern. "Knock it off, sir. He's faithful."

"Sorry, just ribbing you."

Rodriguez stared out the window, every word dripping with loneliness as she said, "Sends me pictures of little Daisy every day. Can't wait for the next leave. Miss them both, a lot."

"I bet."

The convoy entered a small town with some buildings left in ruins after a bombing raid six months ago. It was always at times like these that Malcolm became extra alert, observing everything around him.

Up ahead four women were wearing black Hajibs on either side of the street. One was pushing a pram. That old familiar chill raced up his spine.

"Look alive, Rodriquez," he warned.

"Don't worry, sir, I see 'em."

Malcolm reached for the mic on his tactical headset. "All units be advised, four possible black widows up ahead. Be on alert. Over."

"Roger that," were the replies he received.

Suddenly, two cars pulled out from side exits, blocking the convoy's path.

"All units at the ready. We're being ambushed," he shouted into his headset.

Malcolm was about to plough through them when one woman reached into the pram and swung around, holding an AK-47.

"Look out," Malcolm screamed. He slammed the brakes as she opened fire. Bullets ripped through the glass.

Walsh unloaded on the woman, making quick work of her.

More soldiers filed out of the cars, some carrying handguns and others assault rifles.

Walsh fired on the men, not giving them a chance to retaliate.

The second Humvee pulled up beside them and was ready to attack while the third covered their rear.

A cry in Arabic came from a building to their left. The other three 'women' removed their Hajibs, revealing themselves to be soldiers, also holding AK-47s. Walsh got two while the gunner in the other Humvee got the third. Malcolm and Rodriguez took cover behind their Humvee's doors.

Malcolm looked up as something *whooshed* through the sky. A rocket soared over their vehicle like a miniature meteorite.

"RPG—" he didn't get time to finish warning his comrades as it exploded. It propelled Rodriguez and two of the soldiers in the other vehicles. Both gunners took cover from behind the turret guns.

Seven more insurgents wearing bullet-proof vests and head-scarves, flanked them, raining lead down on the troops.

Blood sprayed from Walsh's head as a bullet connected. The second gunner unleashed a quick burst, taking a few down before being hit himself. Malcolm could tell Walsh was killed as the man fell back and laid still, all life drained from his eyes.

Rodriguez, gotta save her, Malcolm thought, firing, taking care of the soldier on the roof.

Two soldiers from the second Humvee pulled their comrades who were alive to safety while Malcolm covered them. A minute later he did the same with Rodriguez with the others providing covering fire.

Rodriguez's face changed into a canine-like appearance, and black fur took the place of her attractive human skin, as the soldier rolled her onto her back. The woman opened her eyes, now turned luminous green, and bellowed an ear-splitting howl.

Malcolm woke up in his bed, sweating and breathing heavily, and took a few seconds to realize he was in his own bedroom.

Helena stirred, moaning while waking up. "You all right?"

"Yeah...yeah...fine. Go back to sleep."

She rubbed her eyes while asking, "You're having that dream again?"

"It's nothing."

"Still seeing that woman turn into a werewolf?"

Malcolm didn't answer, instead, he looked away.

Helena just stared at him for a moment, an arched brow telling him she wasn't convinced. "You need to get help."

"I'm fine. It's just a dream. Nothing to worry about."

"Whatever." She turned over, returning to sleep.

If only it were that easy to get help, Malcolm thought. He scrolled through some news feeds on his phone for half an hour. This helped him get sleepy. When his eyelids became too heavy to stay awake, he turned the cell off and lay down again.

***

The Boyds' kitchen was something Helena took pride in because she designed it. Cupboards lined up in an L shape on the left-hand side. A shiny silver sink, which was in the middle of a countertop on both sides. Two windows, one at the front and one at the side of the sink, brought plenty of light. The kitchen had a long table covered with a tablecloth showing many illustrations of cups with different types of coffee.

All three Boyds sat around their dinner table, holding hands. Malcolm led them in prayer.

"Lord Jesus, we thank you for the food we're about to eat. May we have enough of it every day throughout the rest of our lives."

"Amen," Helena and David said in unison.

"All right, guys, tuck in," Malcolm said, gesturing to their dishes.

On the table was a bowl of lettuce and another of assorted vegetables. A small, soft, fresh bread roll was on all their side plates while some ham was on their main dinner plate.

"So, Davie, how ya feelin' today?" Malcolm already knew the answer by the eleven-year-old's pallid face.

"Just mostly tired," David said, taking some lettuce and sweetcorn.

Malcolm switched his attention to Helena. "Any episodes?"

"No, none, thank God."

David put a hand up to his mouth as he coughed twice.

Both parents exchanged a glance. Helena took charge of changing the subject. "So, how was work?"

Malcolm was a security guard for a grocery store. They had been burgled three times in the last four months but not since he started there. He was a welcomed deterrent.

"Ah, you know, quiet," Malcolm said while filling his plate.

"But that's good, right?" David asked.

"Yeah, sure is, buddy. No bad guys are gonna try to rob the store when I'm there."

They all shared a quick laugh.

"David got all his homework correct again today," Helena announced proudly.

"Way to go, bud."

The boy sat there, his cheerful demeanor now turning to a frown. "Still don't know why I can't go to school like a normal kid."

Helena took a deep breath to calm herself before answering, "We've been over this, honey. You can't go because of your sickness."

"But it's just so unfair! I can't have anyone over to play with. I never really go out. Why do—" David coughed again, this time blood came onto the center of his palm. He wiped it off with his napkin.

"That's why, bud," Malcolm reminded him gently.

"This sucks." David pushed away his food. "I just want things to go back to the way they were."

Helena held his hand and squeezed it. "I know, hon, us too but we have to make do with the way things are. I know it's hard but—"

David threw his napkin on the table and marched to his room.

"Hey, come back here and finish your meal," Malcolm barked.

"Don't want it," David shouted from down the hall before slamming his bedroom door.

Malcolm clenched both fists. He was about to stand up when Helena caught his arm. "Don't. It's just the hormones. This isn't easy for him."

"It's not easy for any of us, Helena. I know it sucks what he's going through, but we can't let him have an attitude like that."

"He'll calm down. Just let him be."

Malcolm exhaled a frustrated breath and took a bite of his ham.

Helena sipped some red wine from her glass and wiped her mouth with a napkin. "I'll go check on him." She squeezed Malcolm's shoulder as she got up. He waited for his wife to leave the kitchen to shake his head in incredulity.

Over a year ago, things were different. David was going to school, playing with his friends. Helena's and Malcolm's sex life was better than it had ever been. Life itself was pure bliss...until that attack. Now his family were living in the *Twilight Zone*, seemingly forever trapped there. David's Anemia had gotten worse since that encounter. The stress aggravated it.

Helena walked briskly into the kitchen, grabbing a cloth from a drawer, and running it under cold water.

"What's wrong?" Malcolm asked.

"David just broke out in a fever. He's sweating like a pig." She turned off the faucet.

"I'll come with you."

Helena entered first, sat on the bed, and pressed the cold cloth to David's forehead. She stroked his hair while saying, "It's okay, mama's here. Everything's gonna be fine."

Malcolm lowered his head, hating the feeling of utter helplessness. "Your mom's right. You're gonna be okay. We promise."

David nodded at him, his eyes welling up.

"Stay tough, son, stay tough," Malcolm said, ruffling the boy's hair. "I'll be in the kitchen," he told Helena.

Malcolm paced back and forth, waiting for her to enter. *There has to be another way of handling this.*

She shut the door, stress creases forming on her brow. "I know what you're gonna say."

"Do you? Good, so what are we gonna do about it? When can we take him to a proper doctor?"

"You know there's no point. They can't help him."

"Well, we gotta do *something*. Anything is better than what we're doing." Malcolm ran a hand through his hair, feeling the anger bubbling up inside. "I'm going for a smoke."

He walked past Helena without looking at her. He shut the door, breathing in the night's cold, crisp air. Malcolm removed a cigarette from a small box and lit it up. After taking a long drag, he blew out the smoke, and with both eyes shut, he savored the relaxing feeling that flooded his body. The tension in his shoulders eased.

Malcolm grinned, remembering when David was younger before he became Anemic. They'd go to the park together on a Saturday. He'd train him how to catch a ball and how to do a long throw. When he was seven, Malcolm bought him a baseball bat. The first two Saturdays there wasn't much progress with David missing more than he hit. Then on the third, the boy came into his stride, hitting several home runs. On one occasion, David hit the ball so far with the bat that Malcolm thought it was lost. They spent over an hour looking for it. Some old lady found the ball camouflaged in an overgrown bush as she was walking past them. He chuckled recalling the relief on his son's face. David's eyes were filled with pure joy that day, something he missed seeing now.

A cat yowling brought him out of his daydreaming. A stray who he nicknamed Missy, who called from time to time, sat in the middle of the driveway, licking her lips. Her fur was black and white. She had a penchant for fried mincemeat. She wandered over to him, rubbing off his leg.

"Sorry, Missy, you're out of luck tonight."

Suddenly she became spooked, fleeing the yard.

"Hey, where are you go—" Malcolm froze.

Something cold and metallic was pressed against the side of his head. He knew it all too well from his army days. It was the nozzle of a gun. The *click* of a safety being removed confirmed this.

***

Malcolm walked into the house with his hands raised.

Helena, with her back turned to him began saying, "Did you enjoy your—" She screamed as she saw a taller man behind her husband aiming a gun at his head.

"Mom, is everything okay?" David shouted from his room.

"Oh Christ, they have a kid," the tall man with the gun whispered.

A purple-haired woman took out one of her own, nudging it against Helena's jaw. "Tell him everything's fine and we're just friends visiting. Got it?"

Helena nodded, eyeing the weapon nervously. "Ev-everything's fine, honey. Go back to sleep."

"Are you sure?"

"Yes, now go to sleep."

A third man with a skinnier frame who shut the door spoke. "Nat, Stephen, can I speak to you guys for a sec'?"

"Sit down, both of you, *now*. Don't move," the thug named Stephen said.

Malcolm and Helena complied, sitting at the dinner table. He held his wife's hand to comfort her.

"I'm not so sure about us being here," the thin guy said. "They have a kid."

"We got nowhere else to lie low for a few days until we get another ride. There's no other house around for miles."

Stephen spoke up. "I agree with Natalie. It's not like we can book into a B&B now, is it?"

"Yeah, but still. I don't want anyone to get hurt."

Natalie turned to Malcolm and Helena. "Well, if they do what they're told, we can all come out of this in one piece. But if they wanna give us trouble..." She raised the gun, moving it between him and his wife, "Then somebody's gonna get hurt...and it isn't gonna be one of us. Yeah?"

Helena cowered, raising both hands to cover her head. "We'll do as you say. Just don't hurt us."

Natalie stared back at the thin man. "Does that answer your question, Jers?"

"Yeah, it does. Just take it easy, all right?" Jeremy said.

"Don't worry about me, man. If they play along, everything's going to be grand," Natalie answered.

David's violent coughing made everyone stare in the direction of his room.

"Can I go to him? He needs me," Helena asked in a meek voice.

The two men shared a quick glance at one another and then at Natalie. Stephen nodded.

As Helena got up, he added, "Don't try anything, or else your husband will be dead when you come back."

Helena held her hands up as she replied, "Okay...okay. I won't do anything dumb."

He stepped aside to let her pass.

"What exactly is wrong with your son?" Natalie asked Malcolm.

"He has an extreme case of Anemia."

"Did he always have it?" she continued.

"No. He has had it since he was eight, but it got worse."

"Is he on any medication?" Jeremy asked in a kinder tone.

Malcolm swallowed before answering, "Sometimes."

"Oh great," Stephen sighed, "We just had to pick the house with a sick kid."

Jeremy's gaze swept around the room as if seeking something. "Guys," he gestured with his head for the other two to walk to a quiet corner. "We need to get their cell phones so that they won't make any calls."

Stephen nodded. "Good point." He walked towards Malcolm with his hand out. "Give us your phones. All of 'em."

"All right, take it easy." Malcolm handed over his.

"Where's your wife's?" Natalie demanded to know.

"She'll tell you."

Helena came back into the kitchen, casting an uneasy eye on their unwanted guests.

"Is your son, okay?" Jeremy asked.

"Yeah...for now."

"We want your cells. Hubby says you know where it is. Hand it over." Natalie beckoned with some fingers on her left hand to give it.

Helena reached into a back pocket in her pants, placing it in the Irish woman's hand.

"Good girl," Natalie said.

"Is that all of them?" Stephen asked.

Helena and Malcolm confirmed with a nod.

"Great," he added.

"You guys got a spare room?" Jeremy asked. "We're going to

crash here for a few days until we get another car."

"Umm...." Helena's voice trailed off, her eyes focusing on Malcolm.

"We have one, but it's small," Malcolm said.

"It'll do," Jeremy replied with a short, appreciative smile.

***

Jeremy sat at the table, growing ever more uncomfortable, forcing their way into the Boyds' home. He knew it had to be done to avoid the police, but that didn't mean he liked it.

I so can't wait to get out of here. These people are scared out of their wits. His eyes fell on a picture of the Boyds at some holiday resort with the father in shorts and a shirt, donning a pair of sunglasses. Standing beside him was Helena, looking attractive in a pink bikini outfit. Their son, who he learned was called David, stood in the center with some shorts and an inflatable yellow duck around his waist.

The poor kid. Just hope we can leave here with everyone being okay.

"Have yous got any tea?" Natalie asked.

"Erm...yeah, we do," Helena answered.

Natalie got up and rifled through the cupboards for some tea bags.

Jeremy couldn't bear to watch as he felt embarrassed by her behavior. He could see the hatred on Helena's face.

A mixture of mugs hung on hooks under one cupboard. There were Marvel and DC Comics characters on some of them while others had plain designs. Natalie grabbed three. She filled the kettle, flicking it on.

"You want a cuppa?" she put the question to the Boyds. They both shook their heads.

For a few minutes Natalie waited for the kettle to boil and she poured hot water into each mug. A drop hopped onto her hand.

"Ow!" she said, running cold water over it.

This sparked a painful memory from Jeremy's past.

Every Friday Tamara would drop him off at her parents, despite his protests. He hated being there because grandma didn't have a maternal bone in her body, always detesting his presence in not-so-subtle ways. One Saturday morning while she was preparing breakfast, Avril poured herself a mug of coffee.

"So, you play much sports?" she asked.

"No, I suck at them." Jeremy buttered a slice of bread she had baked.

Avril stirred her drink. "You mean you're a wimp?"

Jeremy frowned but kept buttering.

"Well? Are you?" she questioned further, moving closer to him with her spoon.

"No," he answered back abruptly.

"Oh really?" She grabbed his hand, pressing the scalding hot spoon onto his flesh.

"Ow, stop it, Grandma!"

"See? No wonder you suck at them." Harder she pressed it into his soft skin despite him trying to wriggle free. "You're a little pussy!"

Tears now found their way down his cheeks as he screamed, "Let me go. That hurts!"

Avril released her grip. "Geesh. Man up and grow a pair," she snarled as Jeremy ran to the bathroom, crying and running cold water over his burned hand.

From then on, he swore to never become like his grandmother. It was this kind of abuse that eroded his confidence, while making him lose interest in school, despite Tamara's best efforts to encourage him. Many times he tried to tell her about Avril's cruelty, but she never believed him. A few years later he turned to crime when he met Stephen at middle school. Jeremy did his best to avoid being caught by the law but after several close calls, his luck ran out.

Natalie served a hot cup of tea and he thanked her. *After we get outta here and with my cut, I can afford to go straight. No more crime.*

***

Day Two

Malcolm sat up in bed as the early morning sun's rays snuck into their room. He wondered what he could do to get rid of their "guests" without his family being harmed. They had guns. He did too but getting to them would be risky. There was no way to phone the police without their "guests" seeing him. A few months ago he got rid of the landline because nobody used it anymore.

Really wish I hadn't done that now, he thought. *I better get up and check on David.* Malcolm slipped on some clothes. He checked in on his son. The boy stretched his arms, and smiled at his father.

"Morning sunshine. How'd you sleep?"

"Okay, I guess. Who was that in the kitchen last night?"

"Oh...uh, they're some friends we have over. They're crashing here for a few days."

The sound of plates and bowls being taken out from cupboards came from the kitchen. Malcolm knew it was the strangers eating breakfast.

"Is Mom up?"

"No, uh, not yet. That's probably our friends."

"Can I get up too now? Can't sleep anyway."

Malcolm sat on the side of his son's bed. "No, wait a while."

"Oh...all right," David replied in a sad tone, his eyes meeting the floor in disappointment,

"Just wait for me and we can have breakfast together. Okay?"

David nodded, turning on his side to face the window.

Malcolm rose and closed the door, creeping back to his own room. As Malcolm climbed into his bed, his movement woke Helena up and she moaned.

"Hey, can you believe it? They're making breakfast," Malcolm protested quietly.

"Well, what can we do? They got our phones. Calling the cops is out of the question."

"Yeah, I know. I'm just saying."

Helena sat up as she said, "Look, we'll get up and have our own breakfast. I gotta go to town to get some of David's meds."

"Do you really think they're gonna let you go on your own?" Malcolm asked.

"No, but if we get someone to come with me, then they might."

"Helena, they're on the run from the cops. They're not gonna let us go anywhere and they're certainly not gonna risk getting noticed by someone in town."

"Well, you come up with a plan then," she snapped, throwing back the bedclothes and stomping off to the bathroom.

***

An hour later Jeremy was sitting in the kitchen scrolling through a feed on his phone. Helena and Malcolm had just finished eating their breakfast. He felt uncomfortable sitting here, watching them eat. Many times, he'd shift in his seat and cross his legs, never knowing what to do with himself.

"Look, guys, we got a problem," Malcolm announced.

Oh no, what now? Jeremy thought.

"I have a job as a security guard and if I don't go in today, they're gonna want some answers," Malcolm continued.

"Then call in sick," Stephen said.

"I can't keep phoning in sick every day you're here. How long you gonna be anyway?"

"We hope to be out of your hair in a few days," Natalie replied.

"Three tops," Jeremy added to calm Malcolm down.

"*Three days?* I could lose my job if I'm off that long," Malcolm exclaimed.

"Don't they have sick leave?" Jeremy asked.

"Yeah, but I've already taken that when I had to stay with David one week when he was sick a few months ago while Helena was at her mom's. I need this job. It puts food on the table."

"Sorry, but that's really not our problem," Natalie shot back.

51

"You'll just have to pull a sicky."

They heard a door closing down the hall. Helena gave a quick glance to the gun tucked inside Stephen's belt.

"Can you hide that, please?" she pleaded.

Reluctantly he put it behind his back, out of sight.

David gently opened the kitchen door, entering slowly, browbeaten. He kept both eyes on his feet.

"Hey buddy," Malcolm said, trying to sound normal and calm.

Jeremy recognized this as he had to do it many times in the past when trying to steal something.

"Uh...hi." David still didn't raise his head.

Jeremy had to put a hand up to his mouth to hide the shocked expression. Helena had told them that the kid was sick, but the boy's face was paler than he imagined.

Helena spoke up, her turn to put on a brave front. "These are our friends who've come to stay for a few days. This is Stephen, Natalie."

Stephen acknowledged him with a grunt while Natalie feigned a friendly smile.

"And that's Jeremy in the corner."

Jeremy got up to shake David's hand. "Nice to meet you." The boy reminded him of a kid in his neighborhood fifteen years ago. He always looked sickly while wheeling himself around in a wheelchair.

David sat in a seat beside Malcolm, his shoulders slouched.

"I'll get you Coco Pops." Malcolm took a bowl from a cupboard. "Want some fruit with that?"

"Uh-huh," David said in a weak voice.

Helena finished the last of her tea and stared at the three criminals. "Can I speak to you guys outside for a moment?"

They followed her out to the hall, shutting the kitchen door.

"Um, look, I really need to get his meds in town."

"Can't the lad hold out for just a few more days until we're gone?" Natalie said.

Helena gave her an incredulous look. "Have you seen him? David needs his meds, like *today*."

"And we need to lay low until we get a ride out of here so nobody's going anywhere," Natalie reminded her sternly.

"Nat, wait, if he needs them then we have to do something," Jeremy butted in.

"And how do you propose we do that, Sherlock?" Natalie shot back.

"Do you mind if we talk amongst ourselves?" Jeremy said to Helena.

"Yeah...sure." She went back into the kitchen.

"What are you thinking, Jeremy?" Stephen asked.

"One of us could go to town with her to make sure she doesn't rat us out." He saw Natalie rolling her eyes and Stephen's face filling with anguish with each passing second. "I'll go, but we can't let their kid suffer."

"Are you out of your bleedin' mind? Are you actually hearing yourself right now?" Natalie paused, letting her point sink in. "We can't go anywhere because they probably have our faces plastered everywhere. Cops are gonna be looking for us."

"Nat's right, Jeremy. We can't...won't risk losing you and them finding us here."

Time to get tough. "The only reason I took on this job was because you," he aimed a finger at his long-time friend, "promised me that nobody would get hurt—"

"Yeah, well things change, Jers—" Natalie said.

He pursed his lips and fought the urge to tell her to shut up. "I know that, but a kid shouldn't suffer because our plan went sideways. We have to do this."

Natalie ran a hand through her hair. Stephen rubbed his forehead, both feeling the stress of the situation.

"If we agree to this," Stephen started, "how will it work?"

"We could give the mother an hour to get his medicine. I go with her. If we're not back by then, you could threaten something bad will happen to her husband and kid."

"Right, I can go with that," Natalie agreed.

"Wait a second, that means Jeremy putting himself in danger," Stephen objected.

"If he's dumb enough to care for these eejits, let him."

Jeremy took a deep breath and avoided balling up his fists. If Natalie were a man, he'd have punched her lights out a long time ago. "So, we're good to go?"

"If you're insane enough to do it," she replied. "Get the missus out here and tell her."

Stephen opened the door, beckoning Helena. She joined them.

"Right, this is how it's gonna be, yeah? Jeremy here is going with ya to town. You're gonna say he's your cousin or something and he's going in with you to the pharmacist. You got one hour and if ye aren't back before it's up," Natalie pulled up her sweater to reveal her weapon, "I'm gonna start using your hubby and kid as target practice. Got that?"

"Ye- yes," Helena stuttered.

"If anything happens to Jeremy while you're out," Stephen added, getting within an inch of her face and pointing to Natalie he added, "if she doesn't shoot them, I will."

"O- Okay. I won't try anything dumb."

"This entire plan is stupid if you ask me, but he cares about your kid so don't mess things up," Natalie warned.

***

Half an hour later Jeremy and Helena were in the Boyds' new Cherokee 4x4. Jeremy wore a black baseball cap and shades to conceal his identity. He admired the jeep and thought if he ever got out of this situation alive and not in prison, this would be one thing on his "to-buy" list.

For the first ten minutes into their journey, there was an awkward silence. Both didn't know what to say.

Helena cleared her throat, breaking the bout of uneasiness. "Thanks for sticking up for me back there."

"Believe me, I don't wanna do this...but I don't want David to suffer either."

Helena smiled at him. "Well...I appreciate it. You have any brothers or sisters?"

"No. An only child. It has its advantages and disadvantages." Jeremy barely remembered at five years of age, seeing his dad laid out in a coffin. He was caught in the crossfire of a drive-by.

Again, there was no talking for a while until Jeremy asked a question that had been on his mind since he first saw the pallid-looking boy. "Is what David has a lifelong thing?"

"Seems to be. Wish it were different."

"Yeah, I bet."

"It's just last year something happened that scared him." Helena paused for a second as if remembering the event caused her pain. "Now he has terrible anxiety and that makes his Anemia even worse."

Jeremy opened his mouth to ask what frightened the boy. *Maybe I shouldn't. It's none of my business*, he thought.

It was now Helena who bore an expression that said that she had a burning question of her own. "Sorry, but I gotta ask. You seem like a nice guy, so why are you with those creeps?"

Jeremy mulled over his answer for a minute. "I tried going straight, really tried, just didn't work out. Society isn't gonna accept me. All they'll see is an ex-con and not someone who wanted to change. So, I gave up and took this job with a big payday."

"That's if you get out alive."

He nodded while saying, "Trust me, we intend to."

Soon they parked outside the drugstore which had a big window display of hygienic products for both sexes and posters of other items. Jeremy put on his baseball cap, pulling it down as far as he could.

"We gotta be careful here. No funny stuff, okay? If we don't get back within forty minutes, your husband and son are dead. I don't want that, so if anybody asks, I'm your cousin from out of town. Let's go."

Jeremy let Helena lead the way. She pushed open the door and he went in behind her, pretending to be browsing through the men's hygiene section. He kept a watchful eye on her, making sure the frightened mom didn't give a secret signal to alert anyone.

Soon Jeremy's heart pounded a little faster as a police cruiser now parked alongside the Boyds' Cherokee. A sheriff got out, heading straight for the drugstore.

Damn! All right, play it cool. Jeremy calmly walked up to Helena, whispering into her ear, "Sherriff at six o'clock. Hurry."

"I'm going as fast as I can," she replied in a low tone.

Jeremy stood behind a row of shaving materials for men and women, his eyes fixed on the chubby sheriff who stood beside Helena at the counter.

"Hey Rita," he said to one of the staff. "I'm just filling Karen's prescription." The man handed her a pink sheet.

"Coming right up, Danny," Rita said, taking it from him before heading into the back to get the medicine.

He gave a casual scan of the store, soon locking sight with Jeremy.

Oh crap, Jeremy thought, lowering his head, bending down. *Come on, Helena.*

Sherriff Danny made his way to the opposite end of the same aisle Jeremy was in, stealthily glancing down in his direction.

Jeremy straightened up, keeping Helena and the new threat in his sights.

Closer the sheriff moved to him, but Jeremy had reached the aisle's end. *If I move away any further, he's gonna suspect something. Damn it, Helena, move it!*

Sweat leaked underneath his hat. He refrained from tugging at his jacket's collar. Doing so would provoke even further suspicion.

Closer and closer the lawman moved down until he was only three feet away. Unknown to Helena, Jeremy had a pocketknife in one of the jacket pockets. He slowly popped the blade, careful not to cut himself or the material.

Faster his heart thumped and tighter he gripped the weapon when the sheriff was now two feet away. He could see the man casting surreptitious glances at him.

"Sherriff," Rita called out, looking around, holding up a bulging bag of medicine. "Sherriff Danny. Where are you, honey?"

The lawman gave one long, last furtive glance at Jeremy before moving off slowly.

They also gave Helena her bag and she paid for it.

Thank God for that, Jeremy thought, following her out when she left.

***

Seeing Malcolm sitting with an arm around David, assuring him that everything was going to be fine, filled Natalie with a little jealousy. For years she wanted to be a mother and came close too, but God, the universe, whatever cruel celestial being was up there, had other plans.

The father-son bonding moment made Natalie uncomfortable, so she went outside to smoke.

She closed the door, leaned up against the wall and took out her vape. David's laughter and smiles made butterflies flutter in her stomach. It took her back to a time when she was almost an unrecognizable version of herself, living a different life.

The Irish woman had flashbacks of being in her former boyfriend's arms, enjoying nights in front of a fire, each holding a glass of wine while watching a movie. She worked as a temp in a busy lawyer's office and Todd was a handsome marine with muscles any man would die for. She'd lay there gazing into his green eyes for hours. To her, it was heaven. They dated for two years but in the last six months of their relationship, they moved in together.

A week after he had gone back on active duty, Natalie felt nauseous. The mere thought of food would make her stomach churn.

Could it be? She remembered thinking.

The next morning Natalie bought a pregnancy test and brought it home. Those fifteen minutes waiting for the results were the longest in her twenty-seven years on this earth. Tentatively picking up the tube, Natalie stared at the result. Her heart leapt when there was a plus sign.

"Yes," she shouted, wanting to share with the world her news but there was one person more than most that she wanted to tell. Picking up the phone, she rang Todd only getting his voicemail.

57

She wiped away tears before leaving a message, "Todd, you'll never guess what happened? How do you feel about becoming a dad? Give me a ring when you get this." After she hung up, Natalie did a little happy dance before getting dressed for work.

Later that day just before she was about to take her lunch break, the office phone rang. Even now remembering that fateful conversation with his mother made a lump form in her throat.

"Hey Maureen. How's it hanging?"

There was a pause on the other end, broken by a sorrowful whimpering, "Natalie...I got some...." Maureen's voice broke. "Got some bad news, dear. Todd...he's been..."

Natalie left the receiver slip from her hands, her entire world coming to a standstill. The room swayed. She stepped outside for a moment, but fresh air didn't make her feel better. Now the reality of raising a child without its father sank in. No more Todd to kiss or hold at night or to watch their child grow.

Two months went by and one evening when she had finished work, she walked back to her car. A hooded man with a black ski-mask jumped her, punching her twice in the stomach before robbing her handbag. Natalie remembered lying on the ground, seeing the world from a sideways view, watching the thug flee with her wallet and phone.

A few hours later Natalie was in a hospital bed waiting for the results of tests doctors had done on her. After the thief had punched her, she coughed up some blood. One of her friends found her on the ground, dazed and in shock, a little dried stream of blood on the side of her mouth. Natalie remembered a tall doctor standing there with a clipboard, giving the results.

"There's no easy way to say this, Ms. Dolan, but because of the blows your stomach took, I'm sorry, but the baby is dead." She drowned the rest of his speech out. Nothing mattered anymore and she just stared into oblivion, just nodding with lifeless "Yes" and "No" answers.

In the days that followed, she found herself at home lying on the couch with the curtains closed. Minutes passed into hours, and hours passed into days. Her boss had given Natalie two weeks' sick leave. Soon many bottles of red wine dotted her living room and kitchen table. Natalie drank more than she ate.

The morning she was about to return to work, Natalie's mood picked up a little. A busy office would keep her mind occupied, she thought.

But just when she thought the universe couldn't be any crueler, it proved her wrong. An hour into Natalie's shift, the boss, Mr. Thompson, sat her down. He spoke kindly about her recent losses and praised her excellent work. Deep down, Natalie knew what was coming. Her time at the office had ended. On Friday, she'd be without a job. Her suspicions were right. Mr. Thompson gave her an extra two weeks' severance pay to soften the blow, even though it didn't.

To Natalie, it felt like the heartless god sitting on his throne up high, had stuck the knife into an already gaping wound, twisting the blade of fate even more.

Six months had elapsed when one night, while out with a few friends, Natalie met Stephen. It was love at first sight, just like in the movies. He introduced her to a whole new world, mostly one of crime. Of taking what you wanted when you wanted it, consequences be damned. The first few times this appalled her, afraid of being caught. Then she remembered how the world or universe had treated her. Suddenly, she didn't care anymore.

Fuck the world because it screwed me over plenty of times, Natalie remembered thinking. Two months later, she and Stephen, after many weeks of scouting and planning, had robbed a jewelry store, beginning their mini crime spree. Natalie loved every minute of it.

Now taking one last inhalation of the vape, she wiped away the tears and swallowed any ounce of sadness that had arisen from her brief trip down Memory Lane. She was very much in the present, checking her watch.

You better come back in time, love, or your own little slice of heaven will be dead. She tapped the gun tucked into the back of her tracksuit bottoms.

***

Jeremy's amber eyes kept reverting to the digital clock on the dashboard. There were only twenty minutes left to be back at the Boyd house.

"No offence, but can you go a little faster?" Jeremy said, trying not to sound too forceful.

"I'm going as fast as I can," Helena said. "I appreciate you doing this, though. It means a lot. David really needs his medicine."

"I'm just sorry you guys got dragged into this. I never—"

Suddenly there was a loud *bang* like a gunshot. The car swerved left and right until Helena slammed hard on the brakes.

For a moment she and Jeremy sat there, panting, staring out the windshield, both still startled.

"What... the hell... just happened?" Helena screamed.

Jeremy knew what happened but hoped he was wrong. "Stay here. Let me check."

Helena nodded, still trying to catch her breath.

Opening the door, he hopped out. His instincts were correct. Something made the tire burst. A gaping hole was near the bottom of the wheel. Judging by its size, he knew it would take ten minutes to change.

"The tire blew out. You got a spare?" he asked.

Still trying to catch her breath, she threw a thumb over her shoulder. "In... the back."

Opening the trunk, Jeremy took out the wheel and a few tools that were there to change it. *Just hope I get this done in time.*

***

Only two minutes remained. Natalie walked back and forth across the kitchen. Stephen sweated profusely, too. Malcolm could tell that both were worried about their friend. Frankly, he couldn't care less about Jeremy, just wanting Helena home safe and sound.

"Your wife's cutting it fine, isn't she, Mr. Boyd?" Natalie said

60

with an edgy sneer.

"They'll be back. I promise."

"They better be." Stephen picked up a knife he used to cut an apple. "Because if she's not and something happens to our friend," He made a cut-throat motion with the sharp blade. "Catch my drift, dude?"

Yeah," Malcolm said with a large degree of fear, pulling David in closer to protect him. He watched the second hand make its way around the clock. Now only one minute remained.

"I'm telling ya, Steve hon', the bitch did us in. Jers is dead." Natalie reached behind her tracksuit bottom, whipping out her gun. "I say we waste them now, take their car and the money and run."

"No, there's still roughly a minute left. We gotta believe Jeremy's okay."

"Are you for real?" she asked, her voice raised in disbelief. "Open your eyes and stop acting like an eejit. Something has happened to Jers. If it didn't, he'd be here now," She aimed the gun at Malcolm and continued, "with his wife. She ratted on us. Cops could be on their way!"

Stephen brought a fist down hard on the table, meeting her eyes with fierce intensity. "Enough! He'll be back. Just chill."

"*Chill*? Oh, I'll feckin' chill all right when we're so far from here that these arseholes and this house is nothin' but a bleedin' distant memory!" Natalie ran the cold-water faucet, splashing some onto her face. Exhaling a breath of frustration, she dried her cheeks and lips.

Malcolm kept David close as the boy shook with dread and tears rolled down his face. The man gulped when he saw Natalie grip the countertop hard, about to explode in anger.

"You know what," she said, "screw it." She aimed again at them.

Stephen stood up. "Nat, put it away. There are thirty seconds left. He still might—"

"Oh, will you ever get real, man," she spat back. "They're not coming. I'm gonna do what you don't have the balls to." Natalie stood in front of Malcolm, leaning in close, pressing the gun hard into his temple. "And I think I'll start with you. Show Davey boy a thing or two about what the world is really like." She curled a finger around the trigger while turning to David who was now trembling. "You might wanna look away, son, cos this is gonna get messy."

Maybe if I get Natalie alone, I could disarm her and get the jump on the other guy, Malcolm thought. "Can you take David out of the room? Don't let him see this. Do that at least."

Natalie took one look at David and lowered her gun. "Fine. Take him out," she said to Stephen.

Without warning, headlights flooded the driveway, banishing the night's darkness.

When they heard the sounds of car doors being shut after the headlights were switched off, Natalie and Stephen hugged the wall to stay out of sight.

"Stay where yous are and don't say a bloody word," Natalie warned the Boyds. Turning to her partner, she added, "That could be the cops. Be ready."

Now Stephen brought a second gun from inside his jacket, holding it perpendicular to the first. "I'm born ready, baby. Looks like we're shooting our way outta here."

"You're so hot when you talk like that," she said, eyeing him lustfully for a few seconds.

Keys being turned in the front door drew their attention to the hallway. Stephen dashed to behind the kitchen door, taking up a strategic position.

Natalie trained her weapon on Malcolm and David.

The door opened and a voice shouted, "Don't shoot. It's only us!" Jeremy warned. "We're back."

Everyone breathed easy. Natalie and Stephen relaxed their tense demeanors, holstering their guns.

Helena entered the kitchen with a few grocery bags.

"Left it down to the wire, didn't cha, Mrs. Boyd?" Natalie said with a hand on her hips.

"We're back, aren't we?"

"Yeah...just about. Another few seconds and this kitchen

would've gotten very messy...know what I mean?" the Dublin woman reminded her.

"Take it easy, Natalie. We're back," Jeremy said.

Helena threw Natalie a baleful look while placing the bags on the table before hugging her family. "I'm so sorry I'm late, guys. A tire blew out."

"Did everything go okay?" Stephen asked.

"She didn't try anything, did she?" Natalie jumped in.

Jeremy shook his head. "No, she didn't."

Malcolm kept back tears as he embraced his wife and son, just wishing that this nightmare was over already.

***

When Jeremy heard David coughing, he went to his room instead of the bathroom. He knocked twice before entering.

David cowered, crawling further up his bed.

Jeremy stayed at the doorway, holding up his hands. "No, no, it's okay. I'm not going to hurt you. I just heard coughing and wanted to see if you're all right."

"Ye...yeah." David got out of his bed, now retreating to the wall. "Just...a bad cough."

"Okay, well your mom got medicine today so you should be better. I'm just going to take one step in, that's all, so don't be afraid."

David remained motionless, just watching the man's every move.

Jeremy took another step, now coming inside the room. "Sorry about my friends. I know they can be mean sometimes."

"They...almost killed...my dad today."

When he saw David's lips quivering and eyes almost welling up, his head fell to his chest in shame. Never did Jeremy want to hurt or scare any kid. That wasn't part of the plan. "I'm sorry, David, really I am."

He got an idea of how to change the subject by looking at superhero posters, action figures, and comics on the dressing table and floor.

"You like comics, huh?"

"Yeah...guess so," David replied.

Jeremy picked up a Shazam graphic novel. "I loved Wolverine, Batman, and Avengers stories when I was a kid. Who's your favorite hero?"

David took two tentative steps forward, his tense shoulders a little relaxed. "I like Spider-man. Captain America is okay too."

"What about Hawkeye?" When David drew him a blank expression, Jeremy elaborated. "You know, the guy with the cool bow and arrows?"

"Oh..him...yeah he sucks."

Jeremy gave a brief chuckle. "Did you see all the Marvel movies?"

"Most of 'em. Dad and I watch them together."

"I like 'em too." Jeremy put down the graphic novel. "You're a cool kid David, and lucky to have a great mom and dad."

"Um...thanks." David returned a nervous grin.

"Jeremy..." Helena said in a displeased tone that let him know she wasn't comfortable with the man being in there.

"Yeah, I know." He stood outside in the hallway again. "Goodnight, David." He waved at the boy but Helena, who stayed inside her son's room, shut the door.

As he was about to use the bathroom, a thud coming from behind a green door at the end of the hall, made him pause. This door led to the basement. Jeremy moved towards it to investigate further. As he was about to reach for the handle, Stephen called out.

"Jeremy, come on, man. Your pizza's going cold!"

He hesitated for a moment, his curiosity almost getting the better of him but this time his stomach won out.

Taking a seat beside Stephen, his eyes lit up in delight at the piping hot ham, cheese, and pineapple pizza sitting in the table's center.

"Wow, this looks great." Jeremy opened a can of soda and took a slice, putting it onto a plate. "I heard a bang down in the basement a few seconds ago."

"That was probably the dryer," Natalie answered. "Helena said she was carrying clothes down to be dried."

Jeremy shrugged his shoulders. "Oh, okay."

"You weren't scared, were you?" she teased.

"No, just curious. That's all."

***

Soothing music played in the background as Helena lay in David's bed, helping him go to sleep. She stroked his dark blond hair as he lay on her chest.

"Mom, can I ask you something?"

"Sure. What is it?"

"How long will those guys be here?"

"I don't know, but they'll be gone soon."

"What about that man who spoke to me?" David asked.

"Jeremy?" Helena said and he nodded. "He mightn't be as bad but still is one of them."

The boy stayed silent for a moment, but Helena could feel another question coming on.

"Are they going to kill us?" he asked.

She sat him up, looking her son directly in the eyes. "I'd never let anyone hurt you. Never."

"How can you promise that? They nearly killed me and Dad today."

"I know, honey, and I'm sorry about that. I tried to come back really fast. We all just need to be careful and smart. That's all. So just let me and Daddy handle it, okay?"

"Okay, Mom." David stretched his arms and yawned.

"Go to sleep now," Again he laid on her chest, closing his eyes.

Seeing him like this reminded Helena of her younger brother, Mackie, and a day that haunted her for the last twenty years. Ten-year-old Mackie had been playing out in their front garden. Helena, distracted by a conversation she had with a friend on the phone, took her eyes off him for just a moment as he retrieved his ball from the road. The sounds of a car screeching to a halt and

65

Mackie's wailing still resounded in her mind. That evening in the hospital, she sat by his bedside, holding his hands while staring teary-eyed at the boy's fractured legs, both in casts.

"I'm so sorry," she kept repeating.

When David was born and as she held his little pink body in her arms, she remembered making a promise to protect him with her life.

Shifting her body slowly away from his, Helena lay David down on the bed, pulling the blankets up over the boy.

With a steely gaze of determination towards the three intruders in the kitchen, she thought, *Don't worry baby, we'll protect you. We're gonna sort them good.*

Helena marched up to Stephen. "I'm gonna need my phone."

"We already discussed this. No calls in or out, not until we're gone."

"Yeah, so you won't be able to rat us out," Natalie added.

"Well, if our families don't hear from us, they're going to think something's wrong," Helena reminded them calmly.

"She's right," Jeremy said. "We should let them text someone, at least. One of us could be there to watch her."

"Are you on their side now, Jers?" Natalie asked.

"Nat, calm down," Stephen said. "Jeremy has a point. Give her the phone."

Natalie left the kitchen, returning a minute later with Helena's cell. She handed it to her. "There. Now don't get any funny ideas, right?"

"Believe me, I won't. I'm just gonna text my mom."

Stephen stood up, concern all over his face. "Why?"

"We text each other every day. I haven't contacted her in two days so she's gonna worry."

Natalie stayed by her side, keeping a watchful eye.

Helena unlocked the phone. There were three text messages and a missed call from her mother. She showed them to the Irish woman. "See? She's been texting to see if I'm okay. I'm going to reply now." Helena replied her phone wasn't charged and she didn't have time to text back until now. She heard a "bleeping" sound confirming that the message had been sent.

***

Day Three

Jeremy sat at the table eating some Cheerios, something he hadn't done in a while. It was the first morning since they came here that he actually ate some cereal. All this waiting around made him lose sleep at night. He knew Stephen had arranged for a guy to bring them a car and new fake passports to go across the border to Mexico, but things weren't moving fast enough for him. In his mind, this intrusion on the Boyd family wasn't fair on them either.

Natalie and Stephen ate too. His dislike for Natalie was growing more by the day. Stephen was smitten by her good looks and tough Irish attitude, but he didn't seem to notice that she was taking over. Jeremy wondered if she had his best friend under some kind of mind-control spell. Her bossing around was grating on Jeremy's nerves, bringing him closer to snapping when around her.

The kitchen door creaked open. David entered. The paleness on his face diminished, and he looked a lot healthier than normal.

"Hey, kiddo. You look good today," Jeremy complemented him. "How are you feeling?"

"A little better. I feel stronger."

"Guess those meds are working, huh?"

"Maybe...guess so."

"Here," Jeremy got up and pulled back a chair for David. "Sit down. What do you want?" In his peripheral vision, he could see disapproving glances from Natalie and Stephen.

"I'll have some of those." David pointed to the box of Cheerios as he sat on the chair.

"Coming up." Jeremy took a bowl from a cupboard and got a spoon too. David poured a small portion into his bowl and then some milk.

"You sleep okay?" Jeremy asked.

"Yeah...slept good," David replied while munching.

67

"That's great." Again in the corner of his eye, he saw Natalie motion with her head to Stephen to step outside.

"Hey, we're just going out for a smoke," Stephen said. "Can you keep an eye on things here?"

Jeremy nodded. "Sure."

Natalie shut the back door and took out her vape.

"Did you see that in there?" Natalie flicked open her orange lighter. She held the flame and Stephen bent down to light his cigarette.

"He just cares about kids. Always did."

"Maybe he's caring a little too much," Natalie noted.

Stephen took a long drag and exhaled, fixing her with a stern stare. "Meaning?"

"Look, I know he's your friend an' all, but he's becoming a liability. He's getting too close to them."

"Hey, you're damn right he's my friend. He stuck his neck out for me more times than I can count. No way I'm ditching him now."

Natalie held up both hands while taking a step back. "Whoa, easy, cowboy. Nobody said anything about ditching anyone. I'm just saying he's getting too fond of the kid. We have to keep an eye on him."

"Don't worry, he'll be fine. We'll be gone from here anyway in two days."

She took another inhalation from the vape. "Hope your other mate comes through with those passports and car."

"He will. Was talking to him today. Said everything's nearly ready. He leaves tomorrow."

Natalie threw eyes of contempt at the house. "Good. Can't wait to get out of this kip."

"Makes two of us."

***

That night everyone sat around the table as Helena served up dinner - a large chicken casserole with mashed potatoes and vegetables. To Jeremy the chicken's aroma was mouth-watering. It
looked delicious too.

Helena took her seat and held Malcolm's hand. "Let's say
grace," she said.

"Me and Nat don't believe in God. Can't speak for Jeremy,"
Stephen replied.

"I don't believe either," Jeremy said.

"Well, you're in our house, eating *our* food, so this is what we
do," Helena said firmly.

Jeremy saw Malcolm squeeze her hand in caution.

"In case you didn't notice, love, *we're* the ones with the guns."
Natalie waved hers to drive home the point.

"I think that decides that, don't you?" Stephen asked with a
smug grin.

Helena pulled her hand away from Malcolm's as she began eating the dinner, throwing a furtive hateful glance at Natalie.

Headlights shining through the kitchen window as a car drove
into the driveway, made everyone turn their heads.

"You expecting company?" Stephen asked.

"No," Malcolm answered, worry spread across his stubbled
face.

Natalie went over to the window, crouching and peering care-
fully out of it. "It's a sheriff's car!"

Stephen stood up, drawing his gun. "You," pointing a finger at
Helena, "answer the door. Make sure he goes away. If you tell him
anything you shouldn't, they're dead. Nat, Jeremy, take Malcolm
and David to our room. Stay with them. I'll stay in the hallway out
of sight to make sure she doesn't rat us out."

The driver turned off the engine. A door was opened and
closed.

"Come on lads, hurry," Natalie urged them down to their room.
Stephen hid behind a wall in the hallway as Helena answered the
door.

"Evening Sheriff," Helena greeted him, with a little sweat beginning to trickle down her back.

"Evening, ma'am," he said, tipping his hat. He unfurled a poster of the three thieves. "These criminals are at large, and we've reports that they may have passed through our town. Have you seen any of them?"

Helena studied the poster, pretending to inspect it. "No, I haven't seen them at all."

"Is your husband about? Maybe he might've spotted them."

Shoot, what do I say? "No, he's gone out for a while. Won't be back for a few hours."

Sherriff Danny reached into his back pocket and extracted a card. "Here's my number. Be sure to tell him to call me. It's important we get these critters. They're nasty pieces of work."

Helena took the card, feigning interest. She kept her breathing steady. "Oh really? What did they do?"

"Robbed a bank and shot one of their crew in another state. They're armed and dangerous, so if you see 'em, stay clear and let us know."

"Will do, Sherriff."

Jeremy watched Natalie keep a tight hold on David, covering his mouth with one hand while aiming her weapon at his head with the other. A part of him wanted to reassure the kid that everything was going to be fine, but he couldn't do that.

"Don't make a sound," she warned the child.

They heard Helena making small talk with Sheriff Danny, confidently answering his questions.

David squirmed and wriggled to break free. "Let go of me. I can't breathe," he said, though most of it was muffled by Natalie's hand.

"Stay still, you little shite," she whispered, tightening her grip on him. David bit her arm.

"Ow," she said, shoving him away.

"Leave him alone," Malcolm barked in a low voice.

David staggered back, heading towards a bookshelf.

Jeremy tried to catch the boy, but it was too late. He stumbled into the bookshelf, knocking three heavy hardbacks onto the floor.

"Oh no," Malcolm said in dismay.

Natalie brought her gun up, aiming it at David's head. Leaning into his face, she whispered in a menacing tone, "You better hope he goes or you're dead."

Sherriff Danny turned away to leave when he heard a loud crash coming from a room. Helena muttered a curse under her breath.

The lawman turned around with an expression combining curiosity and concern. "Everything all right in there, ma'am?"

"Yes...yes, everything's fine. That's probably just my son goofing around. You know how kids are." She laughed it off nervously.

The sheriff just nodded, his eyes staying in the room's direction for a long moment. "You sure everything's dandy? Nothing you want to tell me?"

Helena could feel the beads of sweat ready to run down her forehead. "Nothing's wrong. We're all good here."

His attention stayed down the hallway for another few seconds before turning away. The tall man who had a hat like JR's from the 1980s TV show, *Dallas*, sat in his patrol vehicle. A minute later he pulled out, heading on down the narrow road leading onto the freeway.

Helena let out a sigh of relief, shutting the door she rested her body against it and breathed easy now. "He's gone."

"Get up there, you little brat!" Natalie pushed David up the hallway.

"Hey, take it easy." Helena brought him to her.

"What happened?" Stephen asked.

"That little bollix made the noise. You're lucky I didn't off ya in there!"

"It was an accident. You pushed me," David spoke up.

"Because you bit me." Natalie showed his bite mark to her boyfriend.

He inspected it. There were no puncture wounds, just a red imprint of David's teeth. Stephen now aimed his gun at the kid. "You know, you're really pushing your luck, little man. Pull a stunt like that again and I'll shoot you myself."

Helena stepped in front of her son. "Over my dead body you will."

"Piss us off enough and that can be arranged, honey," he said with a sneer.

"Look, the sheriff's gone, you're safe," Malcolm interjected, standing between Stephen and Helena. "Just back off from my family."

"Keep them on a tight leash and there'll be no problems," Stephen advised.

"Steve, can I have a word outside with you?" Natalie said, holstering her gun.

"Yeah...sure." He couldn't peel his eyes away as he locked them in a tense exchange with Malcolm until Natalie dragged him out.

Jeremy walked with them until Natalie put up a hand. "No, you stay there. Watch them."

Stephen leaned up against the wall, banging his clenched fist against it. "That was too close, Nat."

"Damn right it was. We need to get out of here, like right now."

"I told you; I'm working on it. He'll be here."

"Well, work faster."

"Hey!" He pointed a cautionary finger at her. "I'm getting sick of you telling me what to do. I'll give him a ring and see if he can speed things up but don't push me."

"In case you haven't noticed, Steve, that sheriff seemed very slow to leave, like he knew something was wrong. I don't know about yous, but I don't wanna end up in the slammer."

"If you got a plan, then I'm all ears," Stephen shot back.

"Oh yeah, I got a plan all right." Natalie drew her weapon. "I say we go in there, shoot them, and take their car, we can hit the highway by midnight."

He pushed her weapon away. "Are you out of your goddamn mind? We can't take their car because it can be traced back to them. In a day or two, we'll have our own and we'll go far away from here."

"And what about the Brady Bunch in there? They'll blab to the cops once we're gone."

"Well," he said seductively, caressing her left arm and cupping her face in his coarse palms, "then we'll off them once we get our stuff. Dead people can't squeal, can they?"

"Oh, I like the way you think."

They both sniggered before sharing a long, passionate kiss.

"But, we have to keep this between us," she suggested. "Can't tell Jers. He's too attached to them."

"Leave him to me. Don't worry, I got you, babe. We'll be home and dry soon."

***

Sherriff Danny parked the patrol unit on the shoulder. His thoughts kept centering on the house. He was sure that the woman was hiding something or someone. She seemed on edge but hid it well. For a while, the sheriff wrestled with a decision and knew it was a step he had to take.

Picking up the radio mic, he pressed the button before speaking into it. "Dispatch, this is the sheriff. I want a unit parked near a house." He called out the zip code.

"Copy that," a young man's voice answered back. "Can I ask why you want one there, sir?"

"Something's mighty off about that place. I want it monitored but from a distance."

"Think they're hiding something?" the deputy said.

"Maybe. Just get one there ASAP."

***

In his parent's bedroom surrounded by a few lit candles, David sat with Malcolm and Helena, joining them in prayer as they held hands together. They knelt while praying. Again, Malcolm led

73

them in concluding the Lord's Prayer.

"And lead us not into temptation but deliver us from evil. Amen."

"Amen," David and Helena chorused.

The boy sat on their bed, feigning calmness under duress, but Malcolm knew deep down his son was afraid.

"You all right, buddy?" he asked him.

David nodded. "Yeah...guess so."

Helena heaped a little praise on him. "He's been doing well since he took his meds."

"Keep doing that and you'll get better," Malcolm reassured him. He studied David for a moment, seeing past the boy's brave smile. In his eyes lurked a certain amount of consternation, hidden behind the innocent gleam of optimism he always tried to portray. "You can always come to Mom and me if you're worried about something."

"Yeah, I know."

Helena sat down beside David. "I know you're scared, honey. So are we, but we'll get through this. Together." She aimed a finger at the door. "They'll be gone in a day or two so don't worry. Life will be back to normal."

"Your mom's right. Everything's gonna be fine. We'll get through this by sticking together. Keep taking your medicine."

Both hugged the boy. He inclined his head towards Malcolm's chest.

Malcolm often wished his own dad would show him the love he craved. There were only a handful of times Dominic, his father, showed any interest or appreciation. Once when fighting with a next-door neighbor and coming back victorious from a fistfight, Dominic said, "See that? That's how you handle things the man's way. You gotta stand up for what you believe in. Gotta be a man." A few years later Malcolm got into a scuffle in school, coming home with a black eye. When asked by 'dear old dad' if he won, Malcolm shook his head, his eyes meeting the floor in shame. Dominic shot a gaze of disappointment at him and walked away, lending no sympathy or support. One of the few times his father ever showed love or appreciation was when Malcolm returned from Iraq. Dominic bought him a beer that day, but Malcolm secretly resented that it took returning from war to show some ounce of pride in his son. Malcolm made a vow to never treat a child of his own like that. And now, he made another private vow to protect his family like he did his platoon and see them through this living nightmare. Even if it meant taking some lives.

***

Stephen leaned against the back wall, enjoying a cigarette as Jeremy joined him.

"Hey man," Stephen greeted him.

Jeremy cleared away the smoke as he said, "We're almost there. Only a day to go and we're home free."

"Yeah...can't wait." Stephen took out the box of cigarettes from his shirt pocket. "Want one?"

"Nah, I'm good, thanks." Jeremy knew by the pensive expression on his friend's face that he was worried. "Do you think your guy will come through for us?"

"Has done in the past. He'll be here. Don't stress, Jeremy." Stephen took one last pull and squashed the cigarette under his foot. "Is that what's bothering you? Getting out of here alive?"

"Well...yeah. I know it's bothering you, too."

"Nah, not worried at all. Damian got me out of scrapes before and he'll come through again." Stephen put an arm around Jeremy's shoulders, pulling him in. "By this time next week, we're gonna be sitting on a beach somewhere in Mexico, sipping cocktails. All this will be in the past. No matter what, I got your back."

"Never doubted that for a second." Jeremy waited a minute to offload what had been on his mind for a few days. "Look, don't take this the wrong way. I know Natalie's your girlfriend," Stephen removed his arm. Jeremy paused for a second, unsure whether to continue, "but I see how she's acting around you lately, kind of taking over."

"She means well and just wants us to get out of here safe and

75

sound. Yeah, I know what you're saying, though. She can overstep the mark."

"I just don't want her to do something that will get us both into trouble," Jeremy said.

"Let me deal with her. I'll talk with Nat tonight and iron out a few things, set a few ground rules."

That should've been done before this job started, Jeremy thought, not daring to voice it.

"Like I said, I got your back. All the way."

"I know. Gotta take a leak." Jeremy walked to the bathroom. He was about to go in when screaming and growling coming from David's room stopped him. Jeremy approached to knock on the door when Helena opened it. She kept it open a fraction when she said, "Don't stay up too late watching the movie. Night." Helena blew him a kiss before closing the door.

"Is everything all right?" Jeremy asked.

"Yeah, he's fine. Just watching a horror movie."

Isn't he a bit too young to watch them? "Oh right. I was just wondering."

She smiled and left. As Jeremy turned to go into the bathroom, the basement door called to him, silently beckoning the man to look inside it.

Nah, he thought while shaking his head.

***

Day Four

In the morning, Jeremy gazed through the slit in the curtains, watching one beautiful ray of sunshine sneaking in. Today, they were going to be free of this place to begin a new life in Mexico.

Stephen's phone vibrated on the locker. He didn't hear it, so Jeremy shook him.

"What?" Stephen barked back, groggily.

"Your phone, it's ringing," Jeremy said.

He became more alert, snatching it up. "Hey, Damo. What's—"

There was a pause, and then his brows met in concern. "Wait, what do you mean you won't have our passports this evening?"

Natalie and Jeremy now exchanged a worrying glance.

"The police stopped you *where*?" Stephen asked, his voice raised in frustration. There was another brief pause before, "Shit!" He threw the cell across the room in anger.

"What's wrong, love?" Natalie asked.

"He's being detained. They stopped him at a checkpoint and the cops found our passports."

"Wait, does that mean...?" Jeremy was afraid to finish that sentence.

"That we're screwed? Yeah, big time." Stephen laid his head back, resting it on the wall.

"So, what're we gonna do now?" Natalie put it to him.

"Guess we gotta go with Plan B. It has to be tonight."

"Wait a second, Plan B? What's that?" Jeremy asked.

"We're gonna take 'our friends' car," Stephen replied, pointing to Helena and Malcolm's bedroom.

"But they're going to be unharmed, right?" Jeremy whispered.

"Sure Jers. We'll just tie them up before we go," Natalie answered in a low voice of her own.

"Sorry Natalie, I was asking Stevie."

She threw him a look of annoyance, which he ignored.

"Yeah, what she said. Nobody's gonna be hurt," Stephen reassured him.

Jeremy could tell by their inability to make eye contact with him that they were lying. He also knew that they wanted to talk in private.

"I'm gonna go to the bathroom. You guys want breakfast?" he asked.

"Not for another half hour. Thanks," Stephen said.

Jeremy left the room but stood outside the door.

"We're still sticking to the original Plan, right?" Natalie pressed for reassurance.

"Yeah...tonight our hands may get wet," Stephen promised.

Jeremy's heart sank. Part of him knew that this was always a possibility. The last thing he wanted was for anyone to die. *I gotta speak to Stevie when he's on his own. Make him see sense.*

***

With a hand on his stomach, Jeremy sat back. It was full from the pancakes Helena had made. Everyone had three each with a large helping of maple syrup, some fruit, and chocolate sprinkles on top. It was the first time in a long while someone made a breakfast like this for him.

"Thank you, Helena, that was great," Jeremy complimented her.

"Yeah, superb. Don't worry, it'll be the last one you'll have to do for us," Natalie said. She and Stephen gazed at one another, sharing a devious smirk.

Jeremy saw Helena noticed it too while slowly taking away their empty plates, casting them a suspicious glance.

"Do you mind if I use your toilet?" Jeremy asked.

"Sure. I don't think there's anyone in there."

The basement beckoned to him again after he finished in the bathroom. *What is it about that damn door?* He knew there was only one way to stop the curiosity calling to him every time he was in the hall. Helena kept a key to the basement hanging on a key rack. Now it was time to put his stealing skills to use.

As she crouched putting dirty dishes into the dishwasher and when nobody else was looking, Jeremy swiped the keys. Sticking one of them into the lock, he turned it. Jeremy entered.

He descended the short stairs. In front of him, there was a tumble dryer, a spare refrigerator, a washing machine, some boxes of toys, and a countertop with clothes baskets. The size of the basement was nearly the full width of the Boyds' kitchen.

At the back, there was a faded poster of basketball legend, Michael Jordan, in mid-air about to do a slam dunk. Just like the basement door, there was something about that area that didn't seem to fit in with the rest of the room. Jeremy examined the poster, feeling its outer edges.

78

As he was almost at the end, he felt something small and metallic. Slipping a hand in behind the poster, he found a sliding bolt lock. Jeremy slid it back and the door opened out.

What Jeremy saw made him gasp. *Holy crap!*

***

As Helena closed the dishwasher door, she heard the cell phone vibrating on her sink. Natalie and Stephen were outside smoking. She kept a close eye on them while checking the phone.

There was an orange, blinking light in the top left-hand corner.

Oh Christ, Helena thought. This type of notification meant only one thing: someone was in the basement. Helena had installed a camera in there, which was connected to an app on her cell. It notified her whenever someone went in. She knew she had to act fast.

***

Jeremy staggered back in shock, gripping the washing machine to keep steady. The door led to another room but what was inside scared him the most.

There were three extra-large dog cages containing shackles in each one. They were big enough to hold humans more than canines. In the last cage was some blood. Jeremy stepped into the room, giving a closer inspection. He went to where the blood was. It had dried, but it looked recent to Jeremy when he scrutinized it.

Who the hell are these people? he thought. *I gotta warn the guys.*

Just as he turned around, something hard hit him across the face. Jeremy fell to the ground, spitting out a few teeth, barely conscious. His vision blurred; the darkness of unconsciousness threatened to overtake him.

Helena stood with a baseball bat. "I'm sorry, Jeremy."

He tried to utter something but could no longer fight, blacking out.

***

Natalie picked up her cup as she sat back down again, feeling rejuvenated after that cigarette. "Can't wait to be out of here tonight."

"I know. Only another twelve hours to go, then we're gone." Stephen drank some of his tea. He grimaced when it had lost its warmth.

"Mine's not as hot either. I'll make a new one. Want another?" Natalie asked.

"Sure."

Natalie picked up their cups. She staggered while approaching the kettle, nausea suddenly hitting her. "Whoa."

Stephen stood up and held her. "Are you all right?"

"Yeah...yeah. Don't know what came over me. I'm fine. Sit down. Relax."

"Are you sure? You're not...pregnant, are you?" he asked nervously.

"Steve," she said, her voice raised in incredulity. "God no."

"Phew, that's a relief."

"If I was, you'd know. Trust me." Natalie emptied the stale water from the kettle and refilled it.

"You mean mood swings and all that?" Stephen said.

"That and more."

"Oh right. I gotta visit the little boy's room." As he reached the door, he stumbled against the doorframe to hold himself up.

Natalie rushed over to him. "Are *you* okay?"

"I... I don't know." Stephen took another three steps and keeled over, falling face-first to the floor.

"Steve!" Natalie began shaking him, trying to rouse him out of whatever this was. "Talk to me. Steve." She looked down the hallway. "Jeremy, come here. Quick!" When there was no reply, she got up.

Once more, the room swayed. Dizziness had taken root. She had to rest against the counter.

Then a wave of realization washed over her. *That bitch put something in our tea.*

Natalie walked like a drunkard down the hallway to their room, moving along the wall for support.

She pushed open the door, rummaging through a bag for the gun. *I'm gonna...sort her.*

When she found it, Natalie's vision blurred, and she saw double.

The sound of the basement door closing made her grin.

"Come here, you. I got something for ya." Taking off the safety again, she moved sluggishly, always leaning up against something while walking out of the room.

Helena stood in the hallway. Natalie aimed the weapon at her. "Just...the one...I wanna...see." Hearing herself reminded Natalie of her younger days getting drunk in Dublin nightclubs. "I don't know what you've done...but you better... undo it."

Helena stood unfazed; her arms folded. "Or what?"

"Do you really...wanna argue...with me?" Natalie waved the pistol. "Cos you know...what I got."

"Oh, I know something. I know you picked the wrong family to mess with."

"Is that...so?" Now there were two Helenas. *Which one is real?*

"Yeah...that's so." Helena checked her watch as she continued, "I also know you're going down in five... four..."

"Going...nowhere...missus." The Irish woman's arms became too heavy to hold up. Those green eyes Stephen loved to gaze into also proved hard to keep open as they grew heavy too.

"Two... one..."

"No!" In a last act of defiance, Natalie raised the gun but let out a cry as her legs buckled.

Helena kicked the gun away and squatted. "Goodnight." She punched Natalie hard across the face, the blow hastening an inevitable outcome.

***

The first thing to hit Jeremy when he opened his eyes was a pounding headache, like a heavyweight boxer was using his brain as a punching bag.

"Oh hell," Jeremy exclaimed when he fully came to his senses. They shackled him and put him inside one of those cages he had seen earlier. A large silver padlock was on the outside. Beside him in their own, with dread painted on their faces, was Natalie and Stephen.

"Welcome back, sunshine," Natalie said, feigning calmness despite the dread in her eyes.

"What the heck have we got ourselves into?" Stephen asked, kicking the cage. "This is worse than prison! There's even blood in mine."

"Ha, worse than prison. I bet that's something you never thought you'd say," Natalie quipped, keeping up the facade.

"They played us," Jeremy said. "I can't believe we fell for the 'friendly neighbors' act."

"Yeah, played us like total eejits," Natalie conceded.

"How are you so calm about this?" Stephen put it to her. "Are you not ticked off about being in this goddamn thing?"

"I am, love, really pissed off, but I tried breaking the lock. No luck."

All three looked up when the outer basement door whined open. They heard two people coming down the stairs. A key turned in the lock. Helena was the first to enter. Behind her was Malcolm, holding a shotgun.

"Well, isn't this a turn of events? You're now the prisoners and not us," Helena gloated.

"Let me outta here and I'll wipe that smile off yer face," Natalie snarled.

Malcolm raised his weapon, aiming it at her. "You might wanna dial it down a notch."

"What did you put in our tea?" Natalie asked. Jeremy could see from her balled fists she was doing everything possible to restrain herself.

Helena gave a proud smile. "Some sedatives. Got them with David's meds when Jeremy wasn't looking. They're tasteless and dissolve really quickly. I knew they'd knock you out within ten minutes.”

“What do you hope to get out of this, Helena? I mean, what’s the endgame here?” Jeremy said.

A sullen expression came upon her. “Despite what you might think, we don’t enjoy this.”

“What are you going to do with us?” Jeremy was almost too afraid to ask.

Helena got on her haunches, meeting him eye to eye. “You’re not a bad guy, Jeremy, just in the wrong place at the wrong time. I’m nearly tempted to let you go...but that’s a non-starter. Can’t have you running off and getting back up to rescue these guys, can we?”

“Just let us go. Give us your car and we’ll be out of your hair,” he pleaded.

“No can do. I know what you were gonna do once you had our car.” She got up, now bending down in front of Natalie’s cage. “You and your beau over there were gonna get your hands ‘wet’, right? Get rid of us, steal our ride and sail off into the sunset. Sound familiar?”

Natalie and Stephen lowered their eyes, both browbeaten.

"Wait, how did you know they said that?" asked Jeremy, his curiosity piqued.

“My dad was in the CIA, taught me a thing or two. I didn’t have bugs but the next best thing...an old baby monitor. I hid it behind the wardrobe.” Helena stood up, smoothing down her light blue skirt. “We’ll be back later to give you your last meal...and then it’s show time.”

“You gonna take us out to the woodshed and shoot us, one by one?” Stephen said, leaning in closer to the door, fixing them with his wild eyes.

“No... something we’d rather not do...” Malcolm replied.

“But don’t have much of a choice. We’ll take no enjoyment in what’s about to happen,” Helena added.

“Then let us go,” Jeremy pleaded once more. “Let us out right now and we’ll go far away from here.”

“Like my wife said, we can’t. We need you guys.”

"For what?" Stephen barked.

"You'll see." Helena with Malcolm left the room, locking the door before walking up the stairs.

"Come back and let us out of here," Natalie roared, kicking the cage and causing it to rattle.

***

Jeremy's empty plate sat beside him. The home-cooked ham and mozzarella pizza was delicious, instantly filling him up. The cheese melted on his tongue. It was the perfect last meal. They had nothing left to do but wait painfully for their deaths. Jeremy sat, clicking his fingers.

"Will you stop doing that?" Natalie shouted. "It's bleedin' annoyin'."

"So sorry, Natalie. I forgot, you're the boss," Jeremy said sarcastically.

"What's that supposed to mean?"

"All right, knock it off," Stephen intervened. "If we're gonna die, I don't want to spend my last hours listening to you two fight."

"Sorry Stevie," Jeremy apologized. "Just can't believe we're here like this. How did we not see the signs?"

Stephen shook his head and sighed. "Don't take it too hard. They had us all fooled."

Footsteps coming down the stairs made everyone sit up.

"Here we go. The moment of truth," Natalie announced with a wry smile.

"Are you not scared?" Jeremy asked.

"I'm not going out crying like a proper girly girl. Won't give *them* the satisfaction."

The footsteps stopped outside the hidden door. Someone turned a key in the lock and pushed the door open. Helena entered and Malcolm was behind her with a hunting rifle. Jeremy recognized it as a .308 Winchester. His dad had a similar one.

"Well, it's time," Helena announced. "I'm so sorry we have to do this but there's no other way."

"Can you skip the monologue, love, and just get to the part where you kill us?" Natalie replied.

"We'll get there soon enough. But first, you'll wanna probably know about these, right?" She pointed to the cages.

"The thought had crossed our minds," Stephen said.

"We use them to collect strays, hobos, and store them here until...well, you'll see in a minute."

Jeremy sat up as straight as he could. "What do you do with them?"

"Believe us, we don't enjoy taking them home and keeping them here until...they're no longer needed," Malcolm answered, a little sadness in his tone laced with shame. "It's more out of necessity."

"So, imagine our surprise when you three came. We just had to string you along long enough for the right moment. Of course, it didn't help when the sheriff called, but thank God he bought the whole act."

Natalie leaned forward, her interest aroused to its fullest, too. "And use us as what? Bait?"

"Oh no, something much more than that," Helena replied, her eyes falling to the floor in sorrowful regret. "What time is it now, hon'?"

Malcolm consulted his watch. "Eleven fifty-eight."

Helena went out of the room and halfway up the stairs. "David, come down."

Again, light from the hall flooded the basement as its door opened. There, little David's shadow loomed to the bottom of the stairs.

Helena beckoned him. "Come here, cutie."

The boy walked slowly down the steps, stopping outside the hidden room. He kept his head low.

"You see, a year ago we had a run-in with some...interesting folk. Let's just say they weren't what we expected. They attacked us but somehow, we escaped...or at least thought we did."

David, with his head still low, began grunting, arms and head twitching.

Helena continued, "We thought none of us were harmed but David got a scratch we didn't see until it was...too late. Our sweet boy was never the same again.

"He was cured of one sickness and got another," Malcolm added.

"Wait a second, you said he was Anemic. Was that a lie?" Jeremy asked.

"No, he really was, but that went away..." Helena's voice trailed off.

"And was replaced by something much worse. He has a sickness no boy should have," Malcolm's voice brimmed with sadness.

David's grunting and groaning became louder, his twitching more violent.

"He became...different, and every thirty days he has to feed," Malcolm continued.

Helena elaborated. "The meds were iron tablets and that sped up the entire process by three days."

"What's happening to him?" Jeremy said.

"Wha...what do you mean by 'feed' and 'speed up the process'?" Stephen asked, fear sneaking its way into his tone, the first time Jeremy had ever seen his friend afraid.

"That's where you guys come in." She stopped as her watch beeped. "Oh God...it's midnight." She and Malcolm retreated as David fell to his knees, bent over, his groaning turning to low growls.

All three prisoners jumped when the boy's bones began snapping, his head twitching vigorously from side to side. Now it arched back, bearing teeth that transformed into fangs.

"What the hell?" Stephen exclaimed.

David's arms grew longer, and more muscular. His height increased too, by twelve inches Jeremy guessed. The boy's shoulders had also become wider and more masculine. As his chest sprouted black hair, his clothes tore apart. His face now morphed into a black wolf's, with penetrating green eyes meeting everyone's gaze. He let loose a ferocious roar, making the three thieves crawl further back into their cages. With heavy breathing, his shoulders rose and fell. The transformation complete.

"As you can see, David's no longer the frail little kid he once was," Helena pointed out the obvious.

"He's a friggin' werewolf?" Jeremy retorted.

Malcolm swung the rifle around to aim it at Jeremy's head. "Don't call him that! He's our little boy. It's not his fault what happened."

"Because David got scratched, he's gotta eat. Once he does, he'll be fine for another thirty days until he gets sick again." She teared up, her lips quivered. "The cycle never ends."

"Ca— can he ch— change into a werewolf at any time?" Jeremy stuttered.

"No, only once a month," Helena answered, shaking her head she continued, "He has brief outbursts closer to when he's about to...turn...but that's it."

Malcolm expanded on her answer, "We think adults can change at will. The guy who made him that way did."

Stephen's face was completely blanched and eyes wide with terror as he asked, "And you're gonna let him...*feed*...on us?"

"You'll be given a sporting chance. He enjoys it more if you make him work for it," Helena informed him. "So, here's the deal, we're gonna let you run off, give you a twenty-second head start. Then we let him loose to...well...do what he does."

"Eat...us?" Natalie said.

"Yes." Helena could not meet Natalie's eyes, her face riddled with shame.

Is this even real? Am I trapped in some messed-up episode of The Twilight Zone or X-Files? Jeremy thought.

Helena stepped out into the main basement and came back with an empty brown beer bottle. "This is to decide who goes first." She stood in the middle of the three cages, bent down to place the bottle on the ground, and spun it.

Jeremy watched it spinning around, stopping at Natalie.

She crawled away from the cage door. "No, please, I'm sorry for all the mean things I did to yous. Please, not me."

"I know this isn't any consolation, but...he'll make it quick."

Helena nodded for Malcolm to open the cage.

"Wait," Stephen shouted. "Take me. It was my idea, let them go."

Helena looked at him with sorrowful eyes. "I really wish we could...but we can't."

"David doesn't need to eat all of us, right?" Stephen asked.

"No... but you'll go straight to the cops, and we can't have that either," Helena replied.

"This way, it kills two birds with one stone. Or in your case, three," Malcolm said.

"We're on the run, remember?" Jeremy reminded him. "The cops are the last place we'd go."

"My son's needs come before yours." Turning to Malcolm, she said, "Go on. Take her out."

"Hold this," he said, handing her the rifle. Unlocking the door, he grabbed Natalie's legs.

She kicked and screamed until he extricated her.

"Hey, leave her alone," Stephen screamed. "Take me instead. Please!"

Helena aimed the Winchester at the woman. "Sorry but follow us."

"Where are you taking her?" Stephen said.

"To the Hunting Ground." Turning her head a fraction to the right she continued, "David, go on ahead."

Now on all fours, he bounded up the stairs like an obedient dog.

Can't believe I'm gonna ask this, but still... Jeremy thought and said in a shaky voice, "How— how is he ab— able to understand you?"

"Don't know...but he does," Helena said.

"I thought you said she'd have a head start?" Stephen asked.

"She will. I'm just getting David ready," Helena replied.

"No... Helena...please don't do this," Natalie begged.

"Move it!" Malcolm ordered, shoving the Irish woman up the stairs.

***

Malcolm once again aimed the .308 Winchester at Natalie as they stopped on 'the Hunting Ground', the Boyds' name for their large backyard. The end of their huge open yard led to a forest. There was a long wall to her left. They painted only half of the wall in white. She wondered if Malcolm got sick of painting and gave up, leaving the rest untouched. Natalie knew since there was no other house for miles, nobody would hear her scream.

"All right, that's far enough," Malcolm said.

Helena approached Natalie. "Here's what's going to happen—"

"Woman to woman, please just let me go. I swear, I won't—"

"Stop! Just stop. Don't make this harder than it already is. You got a twenty-second head-start. I suggest you take it. If you make it to the road, you're free. He won't chase you beyond that point. He's trained to keep away so people won't see him. David, honey."

David stepped forward, grunting while getting on all fours. He growled as saliva dripped off his teeth.

Natalie backed off, taking a quick glance at the forest and one last look at him.

Helena checked her watch. "Your time starts...now!"

Natalie ran as hard and as fast as she could. The last twenty-four hours had drained her mentally, physically, and emotionally. Hell, even prison seemed better now than literally running for her freedom. So, all she had was pure adrenaline.

As she ran farther into the forest, the moon's rays painted all the trees and ground an eerie midnight blue.

David let loose a reverberating howl as she heard him bounding through the field. The Irish woman darted in between the trees, quickly searching for a route to take to the road. As she ran farther, there was an opening in the sea of trees just wide enough to let her catch a glimpse of a road. She set out on the path.

The woman's heightened senses kicked in. Natalie could hear him gaining on her. The pounding of David's paws and his snarling became louder. A branch, broken in half, lay on the ground. She picked up the sharper end of it, a perfect weapon for stabbing.

This could come in handy, she thought, before dashing closer to the road.

The pounding of David's paws and snarling came even closer. Natalie guessed he was less than twelve feet away. Her eyes surveyed every part of the forest, on the lookout for any stones and branches that might trip her up.

Natalie's heart thundered more when the sound of David's running ended. Now leaves rustled in the trees. Branches creaked overhead.

Damn, he's right over me. Digging deep, Natalie picked up speed. For the first time since she started the dash for freedom, she saw part of a road through the dense thicket ahead. It was unmistakable, with the white line going through its middle.

Come on, almost there, she thought, pushing further despite the pain creeping into her ribs and legs.

Natalie gasped as David dropped a few feet ahead, blocking her exit. At first, he remained on all fours for a moment before straightening, his shoulders rising and falling. He licked his lips, clearing the drool from his teeth.

"Woah, ea- easy, boy. I- I- know I was me- mean...but please...don't..." Natalie broke down, her tough exterior fading away. "Don't...kill me."

David grunted once. He opened his mouth while walking towards her, his eyes zoning in on the feisty, purple-haired prey.

"Please..." Natalie begged once more.

Still, he continued walking towards her, his enormous mouth opening wider.

Natalie raised the sharp branch, glancing left and right, filtering the surroundings for a quick exit. Not finding one, she ran to her left.

Again David chased her, taking to the trees, going further on ahead until he landed on one that was smaller than the rest.

Natalie ran, keeping a close eye on him. He dropped as she bolted by. She sprinted around him as he tried to swipe at and knock her, missing by inches.

Natalie, with a rapid glance to her left, could see the road again.

She turned, heading for it.

Louder David's grunts grew as he was closing in, mere inches away.

Almost...there....don't give up, Natalie reminded herself, safety was literally only a few feet away.

As she edged closer, David's panting ceased.

Suddenly something sharp penetrating her right thigh, brought Natalie down. She screamed as a broken piece of branch David launched had protruded through her jeans.

No! So... close. The Dubliner crawled, fighting through agonizing pain. The road and her liberation from this nightmare were less than a few inches away.

David grabbed her left ankle, pulling her away from the sight of any oncoming traffic.

Natalie clung to the dirt, digging her fingers in, but it was futile against the boy's supernatural strength. She roared, kicked, and squirmed to break free, but couldn't.

When they were a respectful distance from the road, David let go of her. He stood over the injured woman, raising his paw. The sharp claws extended even further.

"Rot in hell, freak," Natalie yelled with watery eyes.

He brought the paw down hard, silencing her forever.

***

For fifteen minutes Jeremy watched Stephen cry and punch the cage, kicking the door as hard as he could, trying to force it open. His attempts didn't work. Now Stephen, his energy spent, lowered his head, chin meeting his chest.

"I messed up big time, man. Nat's dead and it's all my fault."

"Hey, you didn't know this was gonna happen. Nobody did," Jeremy consoled him.

"Don't you get it? I'm the one who thought up this job, the one who introduced her to this life. She's now dead because of *me.*"

Stephen stopped crying for a moment and leaned forward. There was a glimpse of hope in his eyes when footsteps came down the stairs again. Only Helena and Malcolm returned.

"No!" Stephen punched and kicked the cage again. "Lemme out of here, you bastards."

Those slow footsteps returned. David walked towards them, what remained of his sweater was saturated in blood, as was some of the fur on his face.

"Nat!" Stephen roared once more, tears flowing down his cheeks.

"You know, I'd almost feel sorry for you if it weren't for the whole holding us hostage and planning to kill us thingy," Helena said.

"We don't enjoy this," Malcolm added. "But what needs to be done is gonna be done."

"But this time, we're gonna change it up. I thought about what you said and you're right, the cops are the last place you'd go. So, we're gonna let you both out at the same time. If one breaks free, then that person can get on with the rest of their life."

Stephen rose his head to meet Helena's nonchalant gaze, his face contorted in fury. Both the man's eyes burned with it. "Once I'm outta here, I'm gonna rip your throat out!"

Malcolm stood in front of her, raising the rifle. "Like to see you try, Steve. Won't get far. I promise you. If this gun doesn't stop you, David will."

Helena tapped Malcolm's shoulder as a gesture to step aside. "Easy honey." From behind her back, Helena took out a pistol. She too aimed the weapon at Stephen. "Let them both out. Don't worry, they won't try anything stupid. I got 'em."

Malcolm handed the rifle to her and then unlocked Jeremy's cage. "Stand over there," Malcolm ordered, pointing to the bottom wall.

Jeremy held his hands up, moving to where he was told to go.

Malcolm bent down, sticking a key into the padlock on Stephen's cage. "I'm warning you, try anything and you're dead here."

"I'm dead anyway."

"We're giving you a fair chance. Take it," Helena advised.

The cage was unlocked. Stephen crawled out, getting to his feet. Jeremy thought he was going to try something, but his friend complied, raising both hands and standing beside him.

"Good. Now follow me and we'll take you to the Hunting Ground." Helena holstered the pistol before leading the way. The two prisoners followed her. Malcolm walked behind them; the rifle also cocked.

The night's air was crisp, a biting chill swirled around them as they stepped outside.

"All right, over there," Malcolm ordered, pointing the gun to a certain spot in the wall.

As they walked over, Stephen whispered, "Remember that stunt we'd pull in high school to get out of gym class?"

"Yeah, but they're not gonna buy that."

"It's worth a try, though," Stephen countered.

"Right now?"

"No better time." Stephen doubled over and moaned, clutching his ribs while feigning pain.

"What's wrong with him?" Helena asked.

"This happens when he's highly stressed," Jeremy answered.

"Not much of a bank robber is he if he can't handle stress," Malcolm jibed. "Get up," he barked. When Stephen didn't, he walked closer, lowering his guard. "I said, get up, jackass."

Stephen leapt at Malcolm and wrestled him for the gun, head-butting him whilst trying to take the rifle off him didn't work. A crack confirmed Malcolm's nose was broken and he cried out. Stephen kept Malcolm's back to Helena, obstructing her line of fire.

David growled and was about to run at the thief hurting his father, but Helena yelled for him to stop.

Stephen kneed Malcolm in the groin.

The man fell to the ground, doubled over.

Stephen now had the rifle. Acting fast, and before Helena could fire off a shot once Malcolm had crumpled to the ground, Stephen fired, hitting her in the chest.

"Oh shit!" Jeremy watched Helena fall back.

***

Deputy Duke Hanlon sat in the cruiser, reading the newspaper. His shift was almost over. Duke had an immense amount of respect for Sheriff Danny, but he felt putting him out here until this hour was ridiculous. Nothing ever happened and the sheriff's theory that the Boyds were hiding people didn't seem plausible. Nobody other than Helena or Malcolm had come out of the house whilst he was on watch.

As he took a sip from his diet soda, Duke heard the unmistakable sound of gunfire. Picking up his cell phone, he dialed Danny's number.

"Yeah?" the sheriff answered, half asleep.

"Sir, there's shots fired at the Boyds' house. Send backup and an ambulance. I'm going in."

This time Danny sounded more alert. "You got it. I'm on my way now."

Duke hung up and drove into the Boyds' yard, leaving the sirens switched off to retain the element of surprise. Taking out his sidearm, he jumped into action.

***

David let loose a ground-shaking bellow before running over to Helena who lay still. An expanding red patch of blood was on her cardigan as the wound continued to pump it out.

Jeremy felt a pang of pity as the boy stroked her hair, whimpering and howling once more into the night.

"No," Malcolm yelled when he recovered from a momentary numbness of shock. Teary-eyed he ran to Helena, falling to his knees, stroking her face, putting both hands on her wound. "No, honey, don't leave me."

Stephen brought the rifle up, peering through the scope. Jeremy knew what he was going to do next.

"Come on, Stevie, let's go. No need for more bloodshed."

"No, man, I'm going to kill that little freak before he kills us."

Stephen moved a finger to the trigger and curled it.

"He's just a kid. He can't help it. Come on, we can make a run for it now."

"Oh, I'll make sure we get away real fine." Stephen's finger now pressed on the trigger.

"No!" Jeremy jumped at him as the weapon fired, missing its intended target.

Malcolm gave a brief yelp as a bullet connected with his throat. The man fell back, arms outspread like Jesus on the cross.

Aw dammit, Jeremy thought. *So much for nobody getting hurt.* Yes, he wanted him and Stephen to leave here alive but not like this.

David ran over to his father, shaking him a few times before releasing another ear-bursting howl of mourning.

"Come on, Stevie, they're down. Let's go!"

"No, I wanna finish this. We're only safe once that kid's dead." Stephen aimed again as David slowly rose to his feet. He tore off what remained of his jumper and pivoted to meet them with an even more ferocious gaze.

Jeremy knew the boy tasted blood already tonight and could see from the deadly gleam in the werewolf's eyes that he would delight in tasting more from the person who killed his parents. He grunted and panted before going on all fours.

"So long, you little runt." Stephen pulled the trigger again...but nothing happened. "You gotta be kidding me!" He hit the weapon and tried once more, but there was nothing but silence. He cursed while throwing down the rifle.

Jeremy saw another figure running from the back of the house. The glint of metal in the moonlight meant this person had a weapon of their own. As the man ran out of the shadows cast by the house and stepped into the light, he could see it was a deputy.

"Nobody moves!" the lawman said. He took one look at the bodies and blessed himself while swearing.

"Oh, buddy, you picked the wrong house to come to tonight," Stephen remarked, panic now tinging his words for the second time today.

David turned towards the deputy, baring his teeth.

"What is this, some kind of freaky Halloween ritual?" the officer asked.

"That's no costume, my friend," Stephen informed him.

"You mean, that's a...?" His voice trailed off as he retreated a few steps.

Jeremy stepped forward in a slow, non-threatening manner. "David, listen to me, I know you can't help this and we're sorry about your parents, but please, don't attack anyone. You're only going to get hurt."

David hissed at him before turning his head back to Stephen.

"I don't know what the hell you are, but keep away," the lawman warned.

David's lips peeled back a little further, baring more of his teeth. Saliva mixed with blood dripped from them. A large red tongue licked it away.

"What are you waiting for?" Stephen screamed.

The deputy gave a warning shot, missing the boy by a few inches.

David, undeterred, growled once more before charging.

"Stop, dammit," the officer shouted. In a moment of trepidation, his finger accidentally pulled the trigger, hitting David in the chest. The boy gave a slight whimper but ran on, determined to kill Stephen.

In a feral scream of his own, the deputy unloaded more lead into the werewolf now advancing on the criminal. David staggered back, clutching his chest, howling in pain. He turned his head towards the deputy and charged at him.

The lawman yelled, firing once more as David lunged at him, landing on top of the frightened officer.

There was silence as Stephen and Jeremy watched on. Neither the officer nor David moved.

"Come on, this is our chance," Stephen said, running towards the house.

"We should just make a run for it. Forget the money." When Stephen ignored Jeremy's advice, he followed him.

They didn't get far as another shot rang out. "Freeze," the deputy roared.

"Oh crap," Jeremy said. Both men came to an immediate stop, holding up their hands in surrender.

Jeremy and Stephen turned around to see the distraught officer rolling David's dead body off of him. He trembled and wept while crawling away from the werewolf whose eyes remained open as well as his mouth with blood gushing from the bullet wounds.

"Oh my God! What the hell just happened?" He sat there, gazing at David, bewildered, his face painted with abject consternation and disbelief. With a shaky hand, he aimed his gun at the two men. "You, s— stay th— there while I ca— call this in." Clutching the shoulder radio, he said, "This is Dep— Deputy Duke Han- Hanlon. I've app- apprehended two murder suspects at the Bo- Boyd house. Dead bodies...everywhere. Send additional med- medical support."

"Received. Second ambulance on the way. Backup ETA in ten minutes. Hang in there. Over."

"You two fel— fellas, stand ov— over there." Duke urged them to move to the wall with his gun. The deputy replaced the empty clip in the weapon.

Stephen and Jeremy walked towards where he pointed.

"Turn around and fa- face it." They did as he said. "Come on, get- get a gr- grip," Jeremy heard the man stammer, trying to snap himself out of this incredulous stupor. "Hands behind your backs."

Jeremy heard the rattling of handcuffs as Duke approached them. He was the first to be handcuffed, his head lowered in ignominy. *There goes my dream of a new life.*

Just as Duke was about to slap the cuffs on Stephen, David grunted and jerked. This made Duke jump back, drawing his weapon again.

Jeremy, in his peripheral vision, could see from Stephen's body language that he was about to make a risky move, exploiting the current distraction.

"Don't do it," Jeremy whispered but it was too late.

Stephen spun around, lunging at the deputy. They both struggled for the gun for a moment, pushing each other back and forth, before it discharged.

Stephen yelled in pain before prying it out of the deputy's hands, shooting the man twice in the chest in quick succession.

Duke fell to the ground, letting out a last gasp of air, his head dropping and eyes closing.

"Oh my God, Stevie. You okay?"

Stephen remained standing there, staring at the deputy. When he was sure the man was dead, he bent down, taking the handcuff keys.

Stephen stumbled against the wall, a hand up to his stomach. Blood spilled through his fingers. "Turn around."

Jeremy could feel Stephen's hands shaking as he tried to unlock the restraints. After what seemed like a few minutes of twisting the key, Jeremy's hands were finally free. Discarding the cuffs, he held Stephen.

"Crap, Stevie, let me go inside and get a towel."

"No... there's no... time." He winced while speaking, his breathing heavy. "Go inside, get the...cash and come...out."

"We gotta stop the bleeding."

"Just get...the damn cash...already!" Stephen insisted.

Jeremy ran to their room, taking the backpacks filled with bank money. He grabbed some towels from the bathroom and brought them out.

Stephen had slid to the ground, his face getting paler.

"Put these up to your wound." Jeremy pressed the towels on his friend's stomach. "We'll take their car and get you to a hospital."

"How are we...gonna explain... this away? We can't. You need...to go."

Jeremy applied more pressure with the towels. "No way, I'm not leaving you here by yourself. We're in this together."

Stephen grabbed Jeremy's t-shirt, pulling him in. "Look at me...does it look like...I can get far? I'll only...slow you down. The last thing I want...is for you," He coughed twice, the second time ejecting blood onto his jeans. "To get caught. You will...if I tag along." He now held one of the bags, shoving it into Jeremy's chest. "Take the money...go...make a new life." Stephen coughed up more blood again.

Jeremy's vision became blurred with tears. "No, Stevie, I'm not leaving you behind. We're bros for life, remember?"

"Yeah...that's why I... want you to leave. You deserve...a better life."

"You can't ask me to do this. You wouldn't if it were the other way around."

"Well it's not...and I am."

"Don't ask me to do this. I... I can't," Jeremy begged, his voice breaking.

"There's no choice. You have to."

Both men turned their heads as sirens sounded in the distance.

"Get out of here. Go!" Stephen urged, pushing Jeremy away.

"I... I—"

Pointing to the road, Stephen shouted, "Go already!"

Jeremy let go of the towel. It slid off. "Please...don't ask me..."

Stephen pressed the gun's nozzle in the center of Jeremy's forehead. "If you don't leave...I'll kill you...myself." Tears fell down Stephen's cheeks. "Don't make this...harder. Just...leave."

"I'll never forget you. Never." Jeremy stood up, picking up the bags. He rummaged through Malcolm's pockets for the keys and found them. He pressed a button to open the trunk, throwing all the bags in. Jeremy slammed it shut, shaking his head while giving one last glance at Stephen.

The wailing of sirens drew closer, throwing shades of red and blue into the dark sky.

Jeremy got in, starting the car. Rolling down the window, he shouted while passing Stephen, "Love you, man."

"Just...go!" He waved him on with the deputy's gun.

Choking down sobs, Jeremy pulled out of the driveway, giving one last glimpse at his injured comrade in the rear-view mirror before speeding away. He drove off into the horizon, leaving his old life and his one loyal friend in a cloud of dust.

Epilogue

Paris, France

Six Months Later

Jeremy sat on the balcony of his apartment, enjoying the warm French sun. He moved here a month after escaping the Boyds' house. When he connected with a buddy of his who was also a well-established forger, Jeremy got fake passports and moved to France. Many times, he wanted to mention his friend as a backup plan to Stephen, but he knew it would be a waste of time. Once Stephen got something into his head, there was nothing that would change his mind.

Ever since he was a kid, there was something about Paris that was alluring to him. Maybe it was the Eiffel Tower, or the way streets were laid out, littered with many cafes. Since moving here, Jeremy learned the lingo quickly and enjoyed the way of life in his dream city.

He picked up the beer resting on a small, round marble bar table he salvaged from a bar owner. The cool liquid meandered down his throat, providing the freshness needed to quench his thirst. He typed up an email on his phone. It was to his mother, letting her know he was safe. Part of him wanted to let her know where he was but deep down, that could never happen if he wanted to stay out of prison. Jeremy sighed while hitting the send button, missing the chats with his mom.

Later he wandered through the streets, soaking in the local ambiance. A pair of violinists played a haunting tune. Their music captured Jeremy's heart as pangs of loneliness mixed with grief hit him every day, especially at night. For three months after Stephen's death, the man's face was all that he saw when falling asleep. Jeremy wished more than anything in the world that Stephen was here, sampling all that Paris offered. Sometimes he'd almost hear his voice calling him. He knew that if Stephen had come to France, he'd probably think up another score. Settling down or taking it easy was never his forte.

As Jeremy passed a costume shop, one thing on display in the window caught his attention. There, on a mannequin, was a plastic werewolf mask. Seeing it now made him shudder. Nightmarish images of David in full werewolf form, howling into the night and charging at Stephen, accompanied an icy chill soaring up his spine. For a few weeks, he mourned the loss of that child too, while also having several nightmares and waking up in a cold sweat.

Poor kid never had a chance in life, Jeremy often thought. His parents were good people forced to do bad things to keep their son alive.

If there was one lesson that incident had taught Jeremy, it was that he never really knew terror, or what horrible secrets this world kept. Now he did, and they robbed him of the closest thing he ever had to a brother.

The Scavenger

Just like Hopps Town, their humble home, Jessica Barlow, Jared Duval, and Adrian Cole are fostering dark secrets. Plagued by loss, cruelty, and physical abuse, these friends are kindred spirits, bound by anguish and elusive dreams. They're soon to find the key to change, but any happy future will demand they face a haunting past and brave a lethal present.

Deep in the forest on the outskirts of town, aging and nearly forgotten, there stands a well from another time. Happening upon this relic, Adrian goads his companions to join him in making a wish. Soon, difficult though it is to admit, their luckless lives seem to shift. The only problem is the changes aren't at all as they'd imagined. Seemingly, they've only left the pan to face the fire.

Should they hope to both survive and thrive, they'll need to pool their wits and draw on mystic inner power. Solving Hopps Town's greatest mystery now means life or death.

"This was a fun YA horror with a fast pace and not too much gore." - Well Worth a Read blog

"Lots of people have played with the "magical wish gone wrong" idea, but Lucid did it with far more finesse and subtlety than most writers […] I hope Aidan will show us more of these three friends in future stories."
-   Gilbert M. Stack

Unlucky Charm

Darkness comes from the most unexpected of places!

Following the events of *The Scavenger*, we now find Jared a year later, on a two-week break from college. He thought this would be a relaxing visit home — then it happened, something so dark he felt a strange sense of déjà vu.

Across town, we find Reggie Danes and Zane Miller, who've been friends for over ten years. After Zane purchases an antique pocket watch, they suddenly find themselves being taunted by past secrets.

Now they must band together to vanquish the demons that plague their lives. Can life ever return to normal? Will the darkness ever disappear?

"If you are a horror story enthusiast, grab your copy now!"
-   Write_Reads

"*Unlucky Charm* is perfect for readers who enjoy high-stakes stories with suspense and scares."
- Priscilla Bettis

Dark Secrets

Dark secrets tarnish their existence, and only the truth can save them now...

When Jessica Barlow finds a knife plunged into her pillow after having a dark, sinister dream, she quickly realizes that it is more than a figment of her imagination. She reaches out to her long-time psychic friend Jared Duval. When Jared makes contact with the knife, he has a vision of a horrific car accident that leaves a woman lifeless at the side of the road.

Jessica and Jared now have to do whatever it takes to uncover the truth and put an end to the mayhem clouding their lives. But what they don't know is that the spirit has joined forces with the malevolent demon, Malik, seeking vengeance on the people who left her for dead – and these people are closer to Jessica than she thinks.

Will they be able to defeat a vicious demon and a vengeful spirit before things take a turn for the worse?

What other darkness lurks in the shadows?

"This was an interesting take on demons, hauntings, possession—you name it from that arena, it was here. All in all, I recommend this to fans of horror and the dark side of paranormal. If that's your thing, this is for you."
-   Mary De Santis

"The plot moves along at an exciting pace. Even Lucid's dialogue passages move the story along as well as help define the characters. Plus, Lucid has a way of describing an action scene that makes you want to duck when a character throws something!

The ending is crazy. I thought the story was wrapping up, but it takes a whole new direction at the end. There's a classic Outer Limits vibe to the ending!

Dark Secrets gets a five-star thumbs-up from me!"
-   Priscilla Bettis

The Lost Son (Second Edition) *

***Winner of the July 2023 Silver Literary Titan Book Award**

Henry Simmons is your average seventeen-year-old kid, until one day he isn't.

All Henry cares about is gaming and ogling his long-time crush, Tracey Maxwell. It feels to him that the universe has granted his wishes when he stumbles upon a mysterious gold coin in his family's garden.

From manipulating physical objects, to getting Tracey to go to prom with him, Henry basks and revels in the power he believes the coin has granted him. Until one day, he finds himself mystically transported to an entirely new dimension, a realm of war and bloodshed.

Henry's life takes a turn as he is trapped in this dimension and given the responsibility of helping to save its people from King Zakarius and his bloodthirsty Sadarkian army. He must fight for the humans in this realm alongside the human king, or he stands to lose his life and his way back home.

While Henry is burdened with this ambiguous task, he makes a few unexpected allies, from former World War II pilots to his neighbor's cat who can now talk. Will Henry and his little troops defeat King Zakarius' army, or will they fail and be trapped in this strange world forever?

"The Lost Son was written by Ireland's own Aidan Lucid; and, let me tell you, he is going to be one of the shining stars in the literary world." - Randy Belaire, author of, "The Reckoning: Chronicles of the Shadow Chaser"

The Lost Son (Second Edition)

Audiobook

Henry Simmons is your typical American 17-year-old kid, who likes to play games, reads comics, and ogles his dream girl, Tracey Maxwell. Henry's life takes a dramatic turn when he finds a magical golden coin. When he learns about the coin's power, the love-struck teenager makes a wish for Tracey to be his prom date. It's granted but soon matters take a turn for the worst. On Prom Night, his date's ex beats him up. While lying on the ground, a drop of Henry's blood falls onto the coin, opening up a portal, and taking him and Tracey to another world.

While there, the two teenagers meet two USAF pilots from 1945 and a talking cat named Jasper. Together they learn that they've been chosen to help King Argoth free his people from an oppressive race of creatures known as the Sadarkians. Not only must Henry learn how to properly harness the coin's power but he, Tracey and co. must learn how to fight and prepare to do combat in an epic battle for freedom. With the Sadarkian army vastly out-numbering King Argoth's, will Henry and his little troop succeed in a world where danger lurks around every corner, and nothing is as it seems.

"I found this to be a fully engaging fantasy novel. From the start, I was pulled into the story, along with the characters, as they explored a world alien to them. With fantasy, I always look to the world-building aspect for rating it. Does the new world just get explained to me, is it just lightly fleshed out? With The Lost Son, the world-building is complex and not narrated to us. We learn as the characters learn, through action and words, not just by being told. It feels like we are on the same journey of discovery as they are, and the elements felt organic. The narration is excellent, the characters are brought to life and each character felt and sounded distinct."

-    Laura Ruetz

The Scavenger Audiobook

Three separate wishes. One twisted nightmare!

Just like Hopps Town, their humble home, Jessica Barlow, Jared Duval, and Adrian Cole are fostering dark secrets. Plagued by loss, cruelty, and physical abuse, these friends are kindred spirits, bound by anguish and elusive dreams. They're soon to find the key to change, but any happy future will demand they face a haunting past and brave a lethal present.

Deep in the forest on the outskirts of town, aging and nearly forgotten, there stands a well from another time. Happening upon this relic, Adrian goads his companions to join him in making a wish. Soon, difficult though it is to admit, their luckless lives do seem to shift. The only problem is, the changes aren't at all as they'd imagined. Seemingly, they've only left the pan to face the fire.

Should they hope to both survive and thrive, they'll need to pool their wits and draw on mystic inner-power. Solving Hopps Town's greatest mystery now means life or death.

About the Author

Aidan Lucid began writing in 2002 after having a spiritual experience. Since then, his works have appeared in national and international poetry anthologies, magazines, and e-zines. Lucid first began working on *The Zargothian Saga* trilogy while recovering from a horrific accident in 2005.

Aidan released *The Scavenger* — a horror novella — in January 2021. The first book in the *Hopps Town* series, it received many positive reviews. He followed that up with *Unlucky Charm* in January 2022 and *Dark Secrets* in 2023.

In July 2023, Aidan won an award (Silver Literary Titan Book Award), for his book, *The Lost Son (Second Edition).* He is also writing more books in The Zargpthian Saga and horror stories.

In his spare time, he likes to meditate, listen to music, and go to the movies with his wife, Claire.

Did You Enjoy the book?

So, what did you think of, *A Beast Within*? Did you like/dislike it? I'd love to hear your thoughts by you posting a review. Each one helps get a book noticed; but it also tells an author what he or she is doing right or wrong, so they can improve their future books. At the end of the day, we authors want to please you guys, the readers. So, please leave a review.

Thank you.

Join My Mailing List

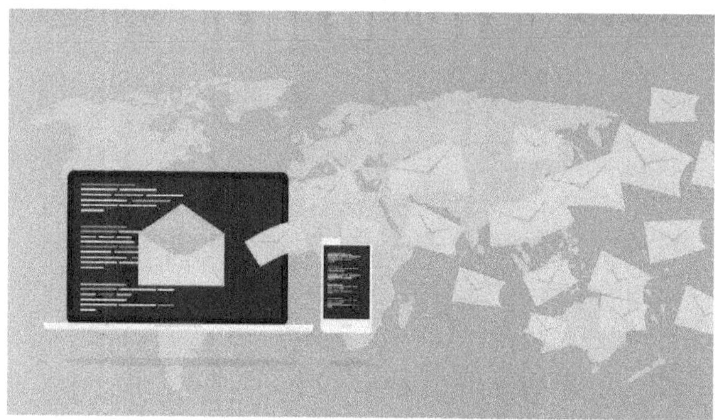

Be sure to sign up to my mailing list today to be notified of the following:

- Upcoming releases
- Free ebook offers
- E-book discounts and special price promotions
- Competitions
- New merchandise

Visit this link to subscribe: https://www.subscribepage.com/hopps_town_mailinglist

Connect with Aidan on:

 https://twitter.com/TheZargothian

 https://www.instagram.com/aidanlucidauthor/